GIRLCOOK

hannah mccouch

GIRLCOOK

a novel

 villard new york

While it is true that the author spent three hellish and insane years working as a cook and that much of the language and many of the scenes conform to the spirit of the restaurant world as she experienced it—with its psychotics, criminals, addicts, sexual misfits, and all—this is a work of fiction. Names, characters, places, and incidents are products of the author's imagination or are used fictitiously. Any resemblance to actual events, locales, or persons, living or dead, is entirely coincidental. The author would like her parents, especially, to understand that the foul language, sex, drinking, and drug use depicted are likewise fictional.

LIBRARY OF CONGRESS CATALOGING-IN-PUBLICATION DATA

McCouch, Hannah.
Girl cook: a novel / Hannah McCouch.
p.   cm.
ISBN 1-4000-6042-7
1. New York (N.Y.)—Fiction. 2. Women cooks—Fiction. 3. Restaurants—Fiction.
4. Cookery—Fiction. I. Title.
PS3613.C383 G57 2003
813'.6—dc21   2002033196

Villard Books website address: www.villard.com

Printed in the United States of America on acid-free paper

98765432

FIRST EDITION

Book design by Carole Lowenstein

For Stephen

ACKNOWLEDGMENTS

No one was more important in bringing this book to life than my agent, Simon Green. Dan Green read the manuscript at several stages and gave invaluable story insight. The enthusiasm, professionalism, and cool of my editors, Bruce Tracy and Katie Zug, helped make this a better book. I am grateful to them all.

Thanks also to: Ruth Davis, Gina Zucker, Sabin Streeter, and Arty Nelson for their friendship and the writing gigs that kept me afloat; Katherine Wessling, Sally Dorst, and the rest of the ladies at *Good Housekeeping* for a day job I could love; Andes Hruby, Linne Ha, Amanda Gersh, Anne Ladd, Danielle Flagg, Janell Hobart, Jennifer Denniston, Whitney Ross, and Charles and Julie Truax, for their inspiration, commiseration, and support; and my brother, Grayson Jonathan McCouch, for his insight into the wonders of the male psyche.

I bow to the Canadian Crew who generously provided companionship, a cell phone, *magrets de canard,* and a well-heated cottage in the Eastern Township woods where much of this book was written: My sister-in-law, Margo MacGillivray; brother-in-law, Ian MacGillivray; Peter Marcotte, and Pat and Mary Trudel.

I'd like to give special thanks to my parents, Donald and Rina McCouch, for going along with all of my harebrained schemes and allowing me to follow my dreams.

This book would not have been possible without the help and guidance of my husband, Stephen MacGillivray, who believed when no one else did, least of all, me.

GIRLCOOK

I've been tossing mesclun greens in the garde-manger at Tacoma for the past nine months, and I'm about to lose my shit. I've been begging the chef to let me give the Caesar salads and cold beet couscous specials a rest and actually cook something for once. I've tried every tactic in the book, starting out by politely inquiring what Noel, the chef, thought the time frame might be on my giving sauté a try. He said that if I demonstrated I was capable of keeping the cinnamon ice-cream boules from melting in the cramped dessert space (six inches to the right of the 500-degree oven), then I could work up some calluses at the grill station. Then, and only then, would he consider putting me on sauté.

Now, no one likes to grill more than I do. But everyone in the business knows there's a huge difference between grill and sauté. Grill guys—and by no means would I want to imply that grilling isn't an art—but grill guys tend to be the cavemen of the kitchen. The guys who don't possess much in the way of artistic flair but can give you a perfectly pink tenderloin of venison after sprinkling it with salt and pepper, searing it, and poking it a couple of times. These are not the men for delicate seasonings and sauce making. They stick to the meat, mostly. And they can take a lot of heat.

Sautéing is the highest station in the kitchen, below the sous chef and chef. And I, for one, goddammit, have piled enough skyscraper salads to be given some consideration. I'm not working my way up the kitchen ladder for my goddamn health. I know all too well the sting of vinegar in an open cut. Oh yes, that salad you're eating as a light appetizer? My bare hands have massaged dressing into every leaf. Lettuce loves me.

But I've got ambition and, I don't mind saying, a decent palate. I believe I'm capable of executing the finer sauce nuances. I want to start my own place. I want to be The Chef. And the only way to do this (aside from buying a place outright) is by becoming the greatest cook I can be. Which means kicking ass on the line, not just salads and desserts. These are my hopes. These are my dreams.

So I'm working dessert and the garde-manger and doing mise en place for the grill guy—butchering and portioning out his New York strips and baking the corn bread that accompanies his stewed goat. This is a good sign. It means I'm in training for the grill station. And what does that prick Noel do? Gets Javier, the dishwasher, to step in and take over. He's priming Javier for the position! Which is a real slap in the face of this Cordon Bleu graduate, I can tell you.

Not that spending a year in Paris learning how to cook from the great maestros makes me an expert—not at all. In no way would I want to imply that the Cordon Bleu was a rigorous or demanding *école de cuisine*, because it wasn't. Out of the thirty or so people in my graduating class, I would say that maybe five intended to pursue cooking as a career, and I was one of them. The majority were wealthy South American girls learning how to cook for their future husbands. Nonetheless, the Cordon Bleu gave me a sense of what was what. I'm willing to concede that a French education may have given me a higher opinion of my cooking abilities than was warranted. But I'm certainly no slouch in a kitchen.

No, this thing with Noel is more a battle of the egos than anything else. Cooking is a very emotional thing. If you have any food confidence or passion at all, you're liable to have a few opinions and theories. And maybe that's the point. Maybe learning how to eat shit is part of the hard-knock lesson Noel feels obligated to teach me.

So I go out of my way to help the new dishwasher stack plates when my station's not busy. My counter space is a testament to anal retention—everything wiped down and neatly in place. I scoop out perfect miniature rock-hard balls of praline and pumpkin ice cream with Pablo, my garde-manger compadre, and manage not to break the wafer-thin chocolate star cookies that perch lightly on top. I work quickly enough to ensure that the ice cream makes it to the customer's table with its structural integrity intact, not slurping around in a big creamy pool.

I do these things above and beyond my normal duties. Which include but are not limited to: blendering up batches of balsamic and Caesar salad dressing; julienning daikon, carrots, and scallions; washing and chopping parsley, basil, and cilantro; assembling the goat cheese, chorizo, and black bean terrine; slicing aged Parmesan; dicing pears; toasting walnuts; peeling and concasseing tomatoes, cucumbers, ancho chilis, and beets.

When Noel told me he was going to be interviewing people for the sauté position, I asked him to consider me. This is the way it goes when you're a woman in the kitchen—you have to beg for everything you get. Write out your speech beforehand. Take a meeting. Most male chefs aren't going to promote you to a station like grill or sauté when they're perfectly happy to keep you in the garde-manger, elbow-deep in greens, making teepees out of black beans. It's been this way in every place I've worked. It's like "You're a woman? I've got a position open in the garde-manger. Take it or leave it."

They want someone dependable (which I am) and ultimately naïve enough (which I suppose I have been) to believe she can work every station in the kitchen, thus training for more prestigious positions. But they don't actually intend to give a girl that kind of a shot.

The most infuriating thing is, Noel's not even a good cook. When pressed, he *can* cook. But nowhere has a starched white chef's uniform substituted so blatantly for an utter lack of talent. Like me, he graduated from a four-year liberal arts institution, so he's not one of those "I was born with a pair of tongs in my hand" kind of guys. Presentation's his forte. A real Jackson Pollock he is, giving the plate an artistic drizzle here, a purposeful zigzag there, and voilà! The master is finished! His head is so big, I swear he has trouble balancing it on his fat little neck. The fact that he's a year younger than I am doesn't make it easier to swallow. But after some psychologizing, I've come to the forgiving conclusion that Noel's ego is just a mask for knowing he sucks, and possibly has a very small penis. To be fair, he's anal. A quality not to be underestimated in the kitchen.

It's kind of a bummer for me though, because really, what can you learn from a chef who can't cook? I just want him to give me a shot on the line. Jesus, you should see some of the incompetents working grill and sauté stations all over this city! It's not a question of whether or not I can handle it. It's that I'm a woman, pure and simple. I know I've got plenty to learn. I just want to be given a chance.

o o o

Jamie's standing by the sink reading the metro section of the *Times* when I come into the kitchen to pour myself a cup of coffee. "Well, look who's up," she says, which pisses me off because she's always jabbing me about getting up late, like I don't work my ass off until one o'clock in the morning.

"Morning," I say, and slide past her to get to the kettle on the stove. As per usual, she only heated up enough water for her herbal tea.

"Sorry, I didn't think you'd be up, and I'm kind of in a rush this morning."

"No problem," I say. But, like, how hard is it to add another cup of water so I don't have to add it cold and reheat the entire deal? I'm totally useless until I've had a cup of coffee, and Jamie knows this but chooses to make me suffer. I think it secretly satisfies her.

"I left the phone and electric bills out on top of the TV. It's all broken down. Just write me a check," she says, taking a dainty bite of a rice cake and throwing the rest in the garbage. She's one of those anorexically thin girls who's always making a big public deal about her enormous appetite and constant milk shake consumptions. I have a bad habit of checking out her ass every time her back is turned. Where is the cellulite? Where?

The paper filter is in the brown two-cup Melitta cone, a quart of whole milk and my heat-saver mug at the ready. The minute that water boils, my life can begin. I don't want to think about money right now. I started buying cans of El Pico because it cost less than half of the Starbucks French Roast I love. I've got nothing saved, and the way things are going at Tacoma lately, it looks like I might not have a job for much longer. Which means I'm going to have to hustle. Which makes me head into the five-by-ten "living area" in search of the Camel Lights.

"You're smoking?" Jamie calls out after me.

"That a problem?"

"In the morning? Yucky."

I don't say anything because I'm too tired to fight. Working in kitchens, some smartass is always taking me under his wing and showing me "the right way" to bake pumpkin or boil carrots, and I don't need my roommate jumping all over me for smoking a cigarette in the morning. Especially since she's a smoker. Admittedly, one of those smoking hypocrites who refuses to smoke until after five, during cocktails and after meals.

"I thought I might drop in tonight with a couple of people from work. Think you could hook us up with some little nibblies?"

This is the way Jamie talks. She is the friend of a college friend who I'd always thought was cool until I started living with Jamie. Then I wondered how anyone I got along with so well could also get along with Jamie. She's got a stick up her ass about three miles long.

"You mean appetizers?" I say, hoping she'll realize they are actual dishes on a menu that people pay money for.

"Yeah, just a couple of things to munch on while we're having drinks," she says, twiddling her fingers to indicate something small and inconsequential.

Jamie works in PR and has come to the businesslike conclusion that life is about freebies—you give me free appetizers, I give you free tickets to some shitty movie premiere. She doesn't understand that what Noel likes even less than a woman in his kitchen is a woman comping all of her well-dressed buddies. The last time Jamie came in with people from work, she kept sneaking up to the window and asking to talk to me, which nearly got me fired. What saved the situation were Jamie's boobs, which were advantageously exposed in a low-cut dress. Javier and Pablo held their hands out in front of them and started pumping their hips back and forth in unison. That made Noel laugh, which basically meant he would overlook my sending out a black bean terrine or two.

"You wearing that to work?" I ask, taking a sip of strong hot coffee. She looks like a pallbearer, and I'm still not over the smoking comment.

"You've got a problem with Armani?"

"Looks like a pantsuit to me."

"Yeah, an Armani pantsuit," she says snootily, flipping her blow-dried salon-blond hair.

"I guess it just depends on what kind and how many 'nibblies,' " I say, holding up two fingers to indicate quotations, "you'll be wanting." Bringing the mug up, I miss my mouth completely and pour hot coffee down the front of my T-shirt, screaming, "Goddamn, mother fuck!"

"Goodness, are you even a girl anymore? I think working in kitchens is starting to get to you."

She got that right, but I'm in no mood, so I say, " 'Goodness'?"

"You know what, Layla? Why don't you just forget it, we'll go to Gotham instead. It's not like we can't expense it."

If you can expense it, bitch, why are you always coming in looking for freebies? is what I'm dying to say. But it's too early in the morning.

I've got to get a new life. I owe $75 on the telephone bill and $15 for Con Ed. This is not good. Especially since I only have $10 in my checking account and won't get paid until next Friday. I hate not paying for things on time, but since I started working as a cook, I've found myself in the position of paying for things late. Julia (my mother) might help me out if I asked her, but I'd rather slit my wrists. She'd use it against me, make me pay in ways I'd find so much more degrading than having Con Ed or Verizon—or Jamie even—ticked at me for being late with my payments.

Before he died, my father was generous with me. But when most of my friends were cashing in on their inheritances, my self-made financier dad sat me down and told me this—"You can't go through life having someone else pay your way. It's not good for you. It takes away any sense of accomplishment you might otherwise have, and it's bad for discipline. I want you to be a success at whatever you do, and I don't think my money can help you do that."

Now, what the hell was I supposed to say to that? I don't mean to bitch, but I was like "Your money is the only thing I've ever had! The only thing that's let me live in the world these last twenty-one years! Your money has helped me in more ways than I can count! And now you want to take it all away? I grew up spending summers on Nantucket and Christmas vacations in Zermatt! I had horses, a great education, designer clothes, and my grandmother's old BMW 528i! I had every advantage, and now you're saying it's not *good* for me? How could it possibly be bad? What more could I want out of life than to have someone else footing the bill? Now I've got to fend for myself? Where's the razor blade? Where? I can't breathe! Oxygen! I need oxygen!"

Julia sent me to a shrink. She thought I was going to do something drastic. Which, I can tell you, when I found out he left all his money to that twenty-five-year-old chippy he left Julia for, was a distinct possibility. I did feel like I was going to die, or at least become a bag lady. I gave heroin addiction some serious consideration. I thought, *Once he sees me withering away, then he'll change his tune.* But you know what happened? He died. In a motorcycle accident in the Swiss Alps. Well, at least he died having fun. I guess that's the most important thing. But it's been a hard thing to come to grips with. A very hard thing. I mean, think of the guilt. It's not like I wasn't wishing him dead after he cut me off. And what happens? A year later, me and his girl, Janet, are sprinkling his ashes off the Grand Teton. At least she paid for the hotel.

As it turned out, he'd established a small educational trust— enough to pay for graduate school. This may sound heartless, but I was like *Yes!* I knew he wouldn't screw me completely. Dad always talked a tough game, but in the end, he was a decent human being. I was twenty-six, and after spending way too much time in Barnes and Noble doing the exercises in *Do*

What You Love, the Money Will Follow and *What Color Is Your Parachute?*, I had an epiphany. It made perfect sense. I loved cooking, eating, and drinking more than anything else in the world—what could be better than devoting my life to food? And where better to learn about food than Paris?

Of course, my father's lawyer and I had a hard time agreeing about exactly what constituted "education" (his interpretation was limited to law and business). Thankfully, I persevered—hence the Cordon Bleu. It was a testament to how badly I wanted a career in cooking. How much faith I had that it was the right path for me. And I had years of dinner-party hosting to back up my decision. I wasn't just grasping at straws. Honestly. Sure, I'd been a bit of a jack-of-all-trades. There'd been a few failed career experiments. But cooking—why hadn't I ever thought of it before? For once in my life, being able to make a living doing something I loved seemed possible.

I spent a year learning how to slice, dice, chop, and taste—perfecting dishes like *boeuf bourguignon, cassoulet, filet de porc vouvray,* and *lapin à la moutarde.* I studied fine wines and the difference between a *brunoise* and a *mirepoix.* I apprenticed with Jacques Vincent at Le Diamond in the Jura Mountains outside of Geneva. I dined at some of the best restaurants in France. I had it good and I know it. Plenty of people would kill to go to cooking school in France. It was the opportunity of a lifetime.

But now I'm back in New York City, working as a salad specialist for a negligible living. Now everything I'd once thought food was about—taste, joy, comfort, making others happy, my own pleasure of creation—has been turned on its head.

o o o

Heading to work at two-thirty on an unusually warm, sunny January afternoon, I'm riding my French beater up Sixth Avenue. Dressed in bike shorts, shoes, and a Day-Glo pink and green polka-dot shirt, I'm riding fast, weaving in and out of traffic—on the out-of-control edge where you have to be if you want to keep your adrenaline up and stay alive. The cabbies are keeping their distance. There are a couple of messengers in front of and behind me. I'm drafting a bus when the driver puts on the brakes. Turning to pass, I clip my right handlebar and am thrown off balance for a microsecond. I don't see my life flashing before me or anything, but my heart's halfway up my throat. I'm three pedal strokes back in business, the adrenaline warming my bowels, when SMACK! See ya!

It all happens so fast, I'm not sure what's going on. Sailing over the handlebars, my feet strapped tight into their baskets, the whole bike comes along for the ride. Crashing down on my hip, the pain is so extreme that I lose myself in the scream. Over and over I'm going, "AAAAAAH! AAAAAAH!" in the middle of Sixth Avenue, the bike a boulder on top of me. Getting ahold of myself, I shut up for a second to consider how hurt I really am. Lying there unable to move for several seconds, it kicks in—*I gotta get the hell out of here, or I'm going to get flattened!*

A young black messenger's leaning over my face, asking if I'm okay. I can hear someone yelling, "Get the fuck over, *rag*-head motherfucker! Pull your *ass* over, you fucking *fuck*!"

"Are you okay?" the guy asks. "Can you get up? Do you need me to call an ambulance? Here, let me get this bike off you."

His hand is on my arm, and he's soothing, seems genuinely concerned about me. This is not the type of thing (the kindness, not the crash) you expect to happen in New York City. Gently, he removes my left foot from the basket—my right had come out in the crash—and picks up the bike. He does this quickly. We're still in the middle of Sixth Avenue, and it feels like we might get run over any second. He offers me his hand, and I grab it. "Let's see if you can walk," he says.

When I'm up, I see a group of messengers standing around me, three are directing traffic. A large Rastaman has physically maneuvered the cab over to the side of the road. He's still yelling, "You stay right *there*, motherfucker. Don't *move!*" He looks at me holding on to my savior's arm and says in a softer tone, "You all right? I saw the whole thing. We can get the police here. This guy tapped your rear wheel—he hit you from behind."

Rastaman's pretty excited. I have a feeling he's got an ax to grind. I'm confused and my hip hurts. There's blood dripping off my elbow, and I raise it to see I've scraped the skin off my lower forearm. The cabbie is shaking his head, saying, "I don't know what he's talking about, I didn't do anything, I didn't touch her!"

And to tell you the truth, I'm not sure whether he did or not, it all happened so fast. It doesn't even occur to me that the only way I could have gone flying over my handlebars was if my rear wheel got tapped. The guy must have hit me. Rastaman is now sitting on the front of the cab to keep the driver from moving. The swarm of messengers is asking me, "You okay? You need a doctor? Hospital?"

I'm walking, even though my hip hurts like crazy. I think I twisted my groin. "I'm not sure what happened," I say. "I have to get to work." I can't think of anything besides the fact that I'm going to be late.

"You sure?" Rastaman says. "You sure you're okay now? Because I saw the whole thing. This guy *nailed* you mon. You got insurance, girl?"

I nod. The first messenger leans my bike against a light post and asks, "You're good?"

I nod again.

"Okay, I'm gonna hit it, then. Here's my beeper if you need a witness or something." He hands me his card, gets on his bike, and rides off.

The other messengers disperse. The Rastaman reluctantly removes himself from the hood of the cab, and the relieved cabbie nods at me and says, "Thank you, miss, thank you," before driving away.

I get back on the bike—pedaling actually hurts less than walking. As for work, I'm going to be late. Very late. It's a matter of pride with me. I've got to be on time. Not to mention Noel, who'll probably stick it on his list entitled "Why I Will Not Give Layla a Shot on Sauté."

Limping the bike through the front door of the restaurant, I slowly hoist it up onto my right shoulder. That hurts. I grab the railing of the staircase up to the locker room. When I enter, Benny and Joaquin, the Colombian bread boys, are standing there in their Calvin Klein underwear. "Whooo, look what the cat dragged in," Benny says.

Slowly putting the bike down, I lock it to a pipe and remove my backpack.

"Oh my *Gaaad*, what happened to you?" Joaquin says.

"I had an accident."

"Jesus, look at your elbow, Mommy. I'm going to get the first-aid kit." Benny quickly pulls on his pants and runs out of the room with no shirt on.

"Will you look at him? Show-off!" Joaquin calls after him. "Now, you sit down here," he says, pulling out a folding chair and leaning down on one knee, "and let *Ho* have a looksy." Lifting up my arm, he bends it at the elbow and gently turns it over, exposing blood and dirt. "We are going to have to get this cleaned up. Come on," he says, standing up. "Put your good arm around my neck and I'll walk you to the bathroom."

"It's okay, Joaquin, I think I can make it by myself."

"You sure? I've been working out," he says, flexing his biceps one by one as he holds his arms out in cradle position. "Jump on! I can carry you over there."

"No thanks," I say, standing up. "Really." A pained "aaah" escapes in one short gasp as I take my first step, and Joaquin quickly sticks his head under my arm.

"You will shut up now."

We hobble together into the bathroom, where Joaquin washes off my elbow and knee with disinfectant soap. Benny shows up at the door with a first-aid kit. "Let me see?" He opens it up and takes the red top off a bottle of Bacitracin. "First a little of this," he says, squirting it all over the bloody parts, "then we dry it off with clean gauze, being careful not to leave any in there." He blows on my elbow and knee, applies Neosporin and finally several Band-Aids. "That should do it."

"Thanks, guys," I say. Part of me appreciates being taken care of like this. The other part feels lame and embarrassed. I don't want to show up in the kitchen looking injured. I want to appear strong, fearless, like I can get hit by a cab on Sixth Avenue and carry on. But the truth is, I feel weak, vulnerable, on the verge of crying. I must have done something to deserve getting hit by that cab. There's always a reason for things.

Alone in the locker room, stripped down to my skivvies, I check out the large bruise that's already changing colors on the side of my upper thigh. *Just what I need,* I think. *An ass accen-tuator.*

o o o

The kitchen is square, with stainless-steel countertops and re-frigerators. White plates are stacked on a rack in the center. Walking through the door, you've got the grill and dishwasher at the back and the sauté station across. Both have gas burners and ovens, which means the grill and sauté guys work facing each other. There's a metal table for plating by the door, with the dessert freezer, salamander (a device used for flash broil-ing), and cold appetizer station opposite. This last section is where Pablo and I work. A pickup window at the sauté station looks out onto the dining area and bar—an open room so small the two are hardly distinguishable. So despite the fact that the *Times* gave Tacoma three stars a couple of weeks ago, the atmosphere is more Benny's Burritos than Chanterelle. That ancho-glazed squab appetizer you're paying fifteen bucks for will be accompanied by Blues Traveler at high volume.

"You're late!" Noel says when I hobble into the kitchen.

"Sorry," I say, "it won't happen again."

In order to get to my station, I have to limp past Noel, painfully pulling my ass forward so I don't rub up against him.

"Rough night?" he asks out of the corner of his mouth.

I'm taking out my knives, and I must be moving in slow mo-tion, because he says much louder than before, "I said you're late, Layla! Light a fire under it!"

I don't respond, but my eyes are welling up. I will not cry. I will hold it together. Pablo, who's been chopping onions with a damp paper towel tucked under his chin to keep from blubbering himself, gets up next to me and says, *"Qué te pasó?"*

"Tuve un accidente."

"Estás bien?"

"Bastante," I say, trying to smile. Lining up my knives—paring, fish, and chef's—I pull out a steel and begin sharpening. I always thought cooks looked so cool sharpening their knives, and it took me a while to get the quick up-and-down, side-to-side motion of it, but I've got it. Now I can pretend I'm a real hotshot. I'm making plenty of quick metal shushing noises, getting my calm back, beginning to focus, dreaming of what I could do to Noel with a really well-sharpened knife, when I notice the new guy.

His name is Danny O'Shaughnessy, and Noel has hired him to work sauté. I hate him from the minute I see him, and not just because I'm predisposed to hating anyone besides myself who gets hired to work sauté.

This blond, spiky-haired, red-faced guy walks—or, I should say, *bounces*—into the kitchen on the balls of his feet, looking like he's just snorted an eight ball. I mean, the guy's hands are trembling, and he's got a layer of sweat on his brow, a couple of white schmoogies in the corners of his mouth, and this "I am one sick motherfucker" smile on his face. He also happens to be sporting an incredibly angry boil on his neck, just above his blinding white chef's-coat collar.

And Noel, Mr. "I know how to pick 'em," Mr. "I'd rather have a coke-snorting prison escapee working my sauté station than some know-it-all woman," is so pleased by my disappointment (which by now is palpable enough for Pablo to put his hand on my arm and say, *"No te preocupas"*), that I'm just itching to stuff my supersized pepper mill up his ass.

Needless to say, this tension does not make for a great evening. The kitchen's hot, as usual, about 95 degrees, and the
first orders are coming in. I've got my pant legs rolled up to my
knees and a blue bandanna tied around my head. Pablo's set
up a bucket of ice with a towel in it for us to wipe our faces with.

O'Shaughnessy seems capable but makes a little too much
noise slamming the oven door and thwapping pans on the
stove for my taste. He's working it, trying to show he's seasoned. But in my experience, any guy who makes exaggerated
or noisy movements is not someone in control of his actions.
Sure, a little oven-door slam here and there when things are
crazy is fine, but when things are slow? It's a display, an act that
everyone else in the kitchen (except Noel, it would seem) can
see right through.

Pablo, not one for verbalizing, is muttering comments under
his breath. "*Maricón, pinche rubio. Sabes? El es de Chiapas,*" he
says, giving me a sneaky smile. Javier is from Chiapas, and it
has somehow turned into the ultimate insult to say someone is
from there.

Orders are starting to roll in, and usually it's Noel who expe-
dites, but he's out of the kitchen for a minute, so the new guy
rips off the ticket, calling out, "Fire terrine! Two mixed greens!
One goat cheese! One Caesar!" And then (and Pablo, Javier,
and I can hardly believe our ears), "*Andale, vite! Vite!*"

I yell back, "Firing terrine! *Dos mixtas!* One goat, One Caesar!" Pablo and I work quietly, throwing various varieties of lettuce into large silver bowls, sprinkling them with salt, pepper,
herbs, and vinaigrette, popping three triangles of black bean
terrine on a flash plate and throwing it under the salamander.
"One duck! Two rib-eye! One salmon! Ordering!"

Javier calls back, "*Dos rib!*"

But the duck and salmon are O'Shaughnessy's, so he doesn't repeat them. Noel comes back into the kitchen. Things are still calm, but it's a Friday night, this is just a warm-up. Soon the whole kitchen will be in a lather of grilling, sautéing, tossing, and flipping.

The orders continue to trickle in. Noel's expediting and giving plates the Pollock flourish. O'Shaughnessy, despite the door-banging and pan-thwacking, is falling behind, so Noel steps in, and like two soldiers covering each other's backs, they begin the sauté dance. Noel's doing the red snapper and skate, while O'Shaughnessy seems to be giving it all he's got to perfect the duck with Bing cherries. This isn't a good sign, but hey, it's his first night. I'm almost willing to give him the benefit of the doubt.

Noel has just started plating his fish when O'Shaughnessy hops up and down a couple of times, says, "Gotta pee," and sprints out of the kitchen, through the dining room toward the bathroom, which is located in full view of the diners. This is very bad.

When O'Shaughnessy gets back to the kitchen, he looks invigorated. I could swear Noel's getting pissed, but I also know he's too proud to admit, after one night, that he made a mistake. Even after having to take over sauté while O'Shaughnessy was powdering his nose. When Noel has to cook it's never a good thing.

Pablo and I are kicking back a little, since most of the room has finished appetizers and are now on to the main course. Soon desserts will be coming in and we'll start up again. Noel looks over at us and yells, "Hey! At least pretend to be working!"

He's looking right at me. Pablo and I act busy, wiping down

our spotless counters and checking our mise en place. When desserts start rolling in, Pablo and I are tag-teaming. I scoop the ice cream, he heats up the chocolate lavas and garnishes with mint. We line the desserts in the window for pickup while Noel rings the bell. He's been pissed at the waiters all night, which is pretty much a constant state of affairs. He hates every one of them. Thinks they're too slow, that they don't care enough about making sure his creations are on the table in record time. And for the most part, his wrath is well deserved. Most of the waiters and waitresses are out-of-work actors, Hallmark-card artists, musicians who could give two shits about whether or not the pheasant is crackling on the outside yet moist on the inside when it gets to the customer.

When Sam, the Tennessee rocker with the Elvis pompadour, finally shows up at the window and starts grabbing flutes of sorbet, Noel's standing like a drill sergeant with his face right next to him, screaming, "You think they want to wind down with a fucking *puddle* of fruit? Is that what they're paying ten bucks a pop for, you little shit?" I half expect him to say, "Now drop and give me fifty ya goddamn cracker!" But Noel tends to be economical with the yelling. I don't think he likes people to see him losing his cool.

Just as Tennessee's turning to walk with the sorbet, Noel grabs the back of his waiter tux coat and yells, "Where the fuck's the mint, Layla?" He's holding up a champagne glass beautifully piled with balls of mango, lemon, and raspberry sorbet. There's no mint on top. And even though I'm sure Noel's noticed that Pablo's on mint tonight, he holds me responsible. He tries to keep his illegal immigrants happy—knows he's got a good deal. They're good workers, and most of them are supporting entire families back in Mexico, Guatemala, and El Salvador, on less than what I get to barely pay my rent. Whipping open the fridge, I thrust my hand into the mint canister and grab a perfect three-leaf sprig. Noel stands there giving me death darts, like *How could you let this happen?* As I'm placing the mint on top of the sorbet, he goes, "Sauté, huh?" And snickers.

Pablo looks sheepish. When I walk back to our station, he says, "Sorry, Layla." And knocks a fist on his forehead several times to illustrate his dismay.

I tell him not to sweat it, I should have noticed it. Besides, he covers my ass all the time, and I'll do the same for him any day. I love working with Pablo. He's quiet, fast, and treats me with respect, which is refreshing. His nickname is *Ratón* and his thick black hair grows so fast he's got to have it cut every other week. He's skinny and five foot three, but his hair gives him another four inches at least. In truth, Pablo hardly ever makes mistakes. He's the kind of guy I'd want working for me if I ever have my own place.

After the mint incident, Noel's on the warpath. He's pissed that the new guy is hoovering lines in the bathroom every half hour and starting to look more crazed by the minute. It kills him that he could be such a shitty judge of character and that all of us are witness to it. Dessert orders are coming in fast and furious, and Noel's barking, "Three sorbet! Two cinnamon boule! Three lava! Four fruit! And I need three petits fours! Do not fuck this up! These are for Oscar's friends!"

Oscar is the owner—a very nice guy. A little below the arm of the law, and who knows if those stories about college boys are true, but he's always friendly to me. Short, with Warhol hair, he wears Clark Kent glasses and holds court in the bar most nights. I can't even get out the door without him forcing me to do several shots of Patrón.

Pablo and I are working in unison—we decided ahead of time who would plate what and have assembled the appropriate glasses, dishes, and plates. We're squirting squiggles of chocolate sauce from a bottle, scooping out balls of sorbet and ice cream, heating up chocolate lavas. . . . There's nothing quite like the feeling of being in sync with someone when you're under the gun and pulling it off. Noel's standing there watching for any slips, any mistakes.

Two by two, we're carrying plates, dishes, and glasses to the pickup window, and the waiters take them away. After setting the final plate on the window ledge, I notice one of the corners of the chocolate star cookies is missing. Noel grabs the plate off the window and holds it one inch from my nose. "What is wrong with this fucking picture?"

I'm already on it, grabbing the cookie container from the shelf and selecting a perfect five-cornered star. Noel's got this Zen thing about odd numbers—it's bad luck to serve things in evens. Those star cookies are like rice paper. You just have to look at one and it breaks. Strange, though, I could have sworn all of the corners were on it when I put it up there. I hear a crash and look above Javier's head to the wall behind the grill station. Cinnamon ice cream and mint are dripping down the white tiles. "Get me another one!" Noel barks.

Pablo's furiously scooping out cinnamon balls while I line up three star cookies—two are runners-up in case one breaks. I deftly squiggle chocolate over the top, perch the cookie and mint delicately, oh, so delicately, and carry the dish, avoiding eye contact with Noel, to the window. O'Shaughnessy puts his sweaty red face over it like he wants to be sure we're doing it right, the boil on his neck staring at me like a vicious red eye. I can smell chocolate on his breath.

"*Ça va?*" I ask sarcastically.

"I don't know, those ice-cream balls could be a little tighter," he says, a serious look on his face like he actually means it.

Noel's chuckling, which is a relief because it means it looks okay to him, but I'm ready to lose it. I can't believe I'm letting this coke-snorting new guy get the best of me. "Yeah," I say, "like marbles. We could name the dish after you." Javier and Pablo laugh. They don't speak much English, but they understand a lot, especially when it pertains to balls.

Noel is not amused. He wants this guy to work out bad. "You want to repeat that?" he says.

"No," I say quietly, because I don't want him madder at me than he already is.

"Well, then, maybe you better keep your fucking mouth shut." The whole kitchen is silent. Noel crossed the line from hardass to asshole, and the public spanking stings. The red tingle flushes my face, and my lower lip is doing that pathetic pre-cry tremble. It doesn't take much these days. I've seen Noel yell at some of the guys, and they seem to absorb it without it ruining their day. I've got a problem. I take it personally. If I were a little more confident about myself and my abilities . . . Well, it's a pretty fine line here in the kitchen. You have to be able to roll with a lot of bullshit but, at the same time, pick your moments carefully before dishing it back out. Make sure the chef is in the mood and you're not hitting too close to a nerve. Bottom line is, Noel wants to be worshiped, not questioned or made fun of. It makes him look bad, and he's got to be the man in charge. I can understand that. But I don't have to like it.

Service is just about over, so I can afford to be a bit of a drama queen. I've got to get out and blow a gasket. Taking off my apron, I want to storm out the door, but my groin stops me quick. Storming is impossible, so I Quasimodo it outside and head down toward the Queensboro Bridge. *How bad can it get?* I wonder. Maybe I'm just premenstrual, but I feel like I've gone completely psychotic. My temples hurt. The tears are running hot down my face, and I let out all the tension of the night. "It's all right, it's okay," I mumble, trying to reason it all out. "It's just a dessert." Then I remember the smell of chocolate on Danny's breath. *That fucking fucker.*

I'm walking by people, aware of what I must look like limping along, muttering to myself in a bandanna, black clogs, checked pants, and soiled white chef's jacket. The night has brought a cool crispness back into the air, and I'm so hot and sweaty that it feels good. "You've got to get hard, suck it up," I say. "Do not let that asshole get the better of you. And whatever you do, never let him see you cry."

There are no people on Second Avenue and I watch the tram head over the East River to Roosevelt Island. Walking west on Sixtieth Street, I notice I'm passing a mental hospital and laugh. Mark Allen, the chef from Mixed Grill, is heading into the Subway Bar. He's known in the local kitchens for making bar rounds during service, slipping in for a beer here, grabbing a shot of Jack or two there. I don't want him to see me. He's always nice to me, but I have a feeling that's just because he knows I wouldn't want to work for him. He can afford to be decent. Crossing the street I do an about face and head back to Tacoma. I wipe my face with the bottom of my jacket and blow my nose in there too for good measure.

When I get back to the kitchen, I'm composed. Noel's gone, and the guys are rifling through their knife cases. Javier's chef's knife is missing, and Pablo thinks he spotted O'Shaughnessy slipping it into his box.

After wiping down the kitchen with paper towels and Formula 409, I sit at the bar with Gustav, the sauté guy from Perla next door. Oscar owns both restaurants, and we share the basement refrigerators and prep areas, which means that Gustav and I see quite a bit of each other. Sometimes he even works lunch sauté at Tacoma.

Dina's tending bar tonight, trying out new marg recipes on us. I like Dina. She's always friendly and not too full of herself. She looks kind of like Cher back in the old days, sporting a permatan and showing skin. I have to say, that sun tattoo around her belly button looks pretty cool.

Gustav sounds like Arnold Schwarzenegger when he talks. "So, ah, Layla, who pissed in your mesclun tonight, eh?"

Can he see that I've been crying? "No one," I say, sulking.

"Come on, baby, I can tell when you're not feeling good. You got your period? Ah?" This is the way it is with Gustav. He has no trouble jumping in with the biological back story.

"Maybe."

"Hey, Dina, a margarita for my menstruating friend here. Better make it a double." Gustav is laughing to himself. "You wanna get high?" he asks, patting the open pocket on his chef's jacket.

"Okay." I don't want to talk, I just want to sit at the bar and quietly sip my drink, maybe take a couple of hits off Gustav's joint, get on my bike, and attempt to ride home.

"Come on. This will cheer you up. I guarantee."

Leaving my barely touched drink on its red-chili-pepper napkin I follow Gustav out the door.

I have never had the hots for Gustav, despite the fact that he's pretty good-looking in an Austrian yodeler way—athletic, with blond hair, blue eyes, a rugged jawline. He Rollerblades to work, and sometimes we go on bike rides across the George Washington Bridge. We have become friends. He's forty, has been cooking since he was fourteen, and knows the kitchen like the back of his hand. Whereas, technically, even after working in three other kitchens, I'm still a neophyte. I've got to keep paying my dues, and I'm not sure how much more I've got in me.

Gustav likes to give me pointers and sometimes this bugs me. It's like, yeah, yeah, I know you're supposed to peel the carrot toward you rather than away, "like a housewife," but I still like doing it my way better. And really, what difference does it make? It's not more economical timewise, so what's the problem? The problem is, there's a cool to maintain in the kitchen. You've got to prove you know how to do things right. But "right" in a kitchen can be a pretty subjective word.

I'm moving slowly down the street, but Gustav doesn't seem to notice. He's too busy searching for the best place to light up. Heading into the shadow of a doorway, he looks around to make sure no one's coming and takes out the joint. We're next door to the Thai Palace, where Gustav's been trying to get into the hostess's pants. "I'm going to marry her," he says, nodding toward the Thai Palace, blowing out smoke.

"You haven't even met her," I say, taking the tip of the joint between my thumb and forefinger and putting it to my lips.

"Her name is Gem," Gustav says, watching me suck in. "Hey, don't Bogart that joint, my friend-eh." He tends to put "eh"s on the ends of his words.

"Where'd you learn that one?" I ask, amused to hear him using Americanisms.

He shrugs. "Don't know. You? Look, you want to tell me what's wrong? Or are you really just on the rag?"

Part of me doesn't want to talk about it. The other part wants Gustav's reaction—concern, shock, anger. "Well, first I got hit by a cab on the way to work."

"Nah!" he says, like this is the worst thing he's ever heard. "Someone hit you with a cab?"

"I went flying. It wasn't pretty."

"Are you okay?" he asks, putting his hand on my arm. Getting closer, he says, "Let me look at your pupils."

"What do my pupils have to do with anything?" He has my head tipped back trying to look into my eyes, his face an inch away from mine. Unable to see anything, he grabs my arm and pulls me toward the streetlamp, where he can get a better look.

"Aaah," I say, because getting pulled in a direction I wasn't prepared for hurts.

"You all right? Jesus, what's wrong with you?" It's like he's perturbed and concerned at the same time. He wants to pull some diagnosis on me. Why do Europeans always seem to have some special medical knowledge that we've never heard about? He's holding my eyelid up with his thumb, taking a good long look.

"Well?" I ask.

"You'll live," he says, stepping back and walking toward the doorway.

He sparks up the joint again and takes a couple of hits to get it rolling before passing it over to me. Sucking hard, I hold the smoke in my lungs a few beats before letting it out. We stand there together for a minute in silence.

"A new guy started working sauté tonight," I say.

"That jackass," he says, referring to Noel. "Didn't he tell you he'd put you on?"

"Not exactly."

"You need to start working sauté, or no one's going to take you seriously."

"Thanks for the tip."

"Hey, baby, sauté's it. Once you're sauté, you can only go up from there."

"Gustav," I say, exasperated, "tell me something I *don't* know." That shuts him up. "So how come you're not a chef yet?" I ask.

"Don't want to be a chef—too much work. And besides, I'm not legal yet—no one will hire me until I get my green card. I entered this green-card lottery thing, you know?"

"They've got a green-card lottery?"

"Yaaaah. And I'll tell you another thing, I'm going to win it."

Widening my eyes, I nod my head, like *What the hell, it could happen.* I'm starting to feel buzzed. "Hey, show me the love," I say, holding out my thumb and forefinger.

"Baby, I show you all the love you need," he says, grabbing my ass with a little too much gusto for my condition before quickly lightening his grip and saying, "Oooh, sorry, I forgot."

I could be offended when Gustav grabs my ass or dry-humps my leg, but that would be counterproductive. It's the way he is, and I don't let it offend me. We couldn't be friends if I did. He's high now, and I'm getting there. I lift up my head on the inhale, and turning to my right, I see Danny O'Shaughnessy coming out of Perla. "That's him," I say, "that's the guy."

"So what you want me to do? Kick his ass?"

"For starters. I swear, Gustav, the guy was hoovering all through service. We think he stole Javier's knife."

Gustav perks up at this. "No shit. He stole Javier's knife?"

"Shhh. He's walking this way."

"And if you think I care whether he hears me or not, you can think again."

"Please, Gustav. I've got to work with the guy."

"So you won't mind if I have to conduct a little whaddayou-callit? Body-cavity search-eh?"

I start giggling. "You think he's hiding the knife up there?"

"Hey, some people like it."

"Come on," I say, "let's go back inside, I'm getting cold."

"He's a scumbag, that's for sure—I can see it in his face. Do you know how many hours Javier has to work to be able to buy his own chef's knife? And this *douchebag*," he says, just as Danny's two feet away.

"That's my name, don't wear it out." Danny's smiling the smile of a man who's got nothing to lose. He's changed out of his chef's whites into a pair of slacks and a blazer. I wonder how a sauté cook can afford such nice clothes. He's carrying his knives in a red metal toolbox with a big lock on the side.

"Danny, this is Gustav," I say, trying to be polite. The introduction seems to have mellowed Gustav out, because he looks at Danny, holds out his hand, and says, "Hey, nice to meet you."

Danny's eyes look like they're spinning around in his head. He's rocking from side to side, wiping the tip of his nose and the corners of his mouth in quick succession. "Correct me if

I'm wrong," he says, "but did I catch a whiff of the mighty ganj? I could really use a mellowing influence."

"Nope," Gustav says. Putting his hand on my shoulder, he says, "Layla and I were just talking knives. She loves her Sabatier, but I say there's nothing better than Wusthof. What's your brand?"

Danny doesn't seem at all flustered by the question. "I use all different kinds. My favorite is this serrated no-name brand that I buy at J. B. Prince—about ten bucks."

"Yeah?" Gustav asks. "You use that as your chef's knife?"

"Oh, I've got a few different chef's knives."

"Hah," Gustav says in that tone that signifies "That so?" Which stops the conversation dead.

"Hey, Layla, sorry for givin' ya shit in there tonight, you know how things get."

"I don't know how things get," Gustav says.

"Well, you don't work in a kitchen, then," Danny says, trying to build up camaraderie with me. He has no idea that Gustav can cook him under the counter.

"I don't?"

"You do?"

"Last time I checked."

"Sorry. You must know what I'm talking about then."

"You mean when new guys with shit for brains get fresh during service?"

Danny starts laughing, but not like he's scared. More like what Gustav said is the funniest thing he's ever heard. In the light from the streetlamp, his angry red boil looks like he's been messing with it.

"Hey, Danny?" I ask. "Do you know what happened to that chocolate star?"

"Oh, sorry about that one. I just wanted a taste and didn't think Noel would freak like that. He's pretty high-strung, isn't he?"

Look who's talking. "Listen, next time you want to taste something, just ask, okay?"

Three black guys in baggy jeans and big, puffy Tommy Hilfiger jackets are walking up the street. "Yo, Danny O!" one calls out.

"Hey, Jamal, what's shakin', bro?"

"I am, brother, I am. You ready?"

"Better believe it," Danny says, and then to Gustav and me, "Been a pleasure. See you tomorrow, Layla."

"Looking forward to it, Danny."

"I bet you are," he says, clicking his tongue and winking.

I drop Gustav off at the Thai Palace and head back to the bar at Tacoma. Halfway through a pink Patrón margarita on the rocks with Grand Marnier floater, I decide that what I could really use is some ice cream.

Dina says, "Hey, how about one of those coconut cookies for your buddy?"

In the kitchen, Pablo and Javier are sitting up on the counter, eating chicken and drinking Cokes. Pablo says, *"Qué tal, chica?"*

I say, "Bien," and head for the icebox.

Javier says, *"Necesitas helado para el culo?"* And smiles.

It's kind of a private joke between us. One time I told him I loved ice cream and he asked me why, and I jokingly said, "For my ass." So now every time he sees me eating ice cream, he says, *"Necesitas helado para el culo,"* and to tell you the truth, I'm getting kind of sick of it. Not only because I don't feel like discussing my ass with Javier, but because I've been eating way too much ice cream lately, and my ass is starting to show signs. It's been hard to stop myself, though. I don't seem to have control over anything—my job, my ice-cream intake, and don't even get me started on my love life. I haven't had one since the short-lived Jura Mountain pastry chef with the Coke-bottle glasses. Didn't look like much when he was putting together the apple tarts but turned into a real Don Juan as soon as the lights went out. He called me his "American Prancess." A master sugar puller—he'd won contests with his swans and delicate roses. He had a way with his hands.

I scoop out a spoonful of cinnamon, and another of hazelnut and crush a chocolate-star wafer over the top. The ice cream has softened from the icebox being opened and closed so many times throughout service and is now the perfect slightly soft consistency. Mushing the wafer into the ice cream, I get up on the counter with Javier and Pablo. The three of us sit there eating in silence. Sometimes I think I could live on nothing but ice cream. It's the best comfort food around.

We're interrupted by Dina, who sticks her head through the window and says, "Who do I need to screw around here to get a coconut cookie?"

"Sorry, I forgot," I say, jumping off the counter and grabbing the cookie Tupperware off the shelf. Javier and Pablo suck on their chicken bones, elbowing each other in the sides like Beavis and Butthead. *She said "screw," huh, huh, huh, huh . . .*

I hand her a dessert plate with three coconut cookies on it. Holding one up, she looks at it dreamily, before biting in and chewing slow. "*That's* what I'm talkin' about," she says, using her pinky to dislodge cookie from her molars. "Thanks, Lay."

When she's out of earshot, Pablo says, "*Esta chica es guapa.*" Javier nods with enthusiasm.

"You guys like Dina?" The both smile and nod. "*Pero estás casado pinche*, Pablo."

"*No le importa*," says Javier, grinning.

"*Perros*," I say.

o o o

Jamie's asleep when I get home. I pour myself a glass of water and check the pad by the phone for messages. It says, "Listen to messages."

There's one from Gustav telling me to sleep tight and not worry about the douchebag. Another from Billy, who's having a party on my night off and wants me to be there.

And then there's Julia. "Hello, sweetheart, it's your mother, remember me? I just wanted to call and see how you were doing, and make sure you know that my show is on tomorrow at nine. I don't know if you work tomorrow night? Well, anyway, you can tape it. It's a good one, some of my best work. I think you'll like it. Don't forget to tell your friends"—beeeep!

I know there had to be more to *that* message. Julia tends to go on. I don't think she understands answering machines too well, which is a major blessing as far as I'm concerned. She's out of touch that way. I have a feeling she probably keeps talking even after the beep. I've heard her mention things that she supposedly left on the machine, which come as news to me. Her divorce from husband number three, for instance. He was a nice one, too—was going to take us to Aspen for Christmas before he caught Julia screwing her assistant.

My mother is an actress on a new show called *Intrigues*, sort of a nighttime soap. She spent all last summer shooting the pilot, and it just started airing two weeks ago. She's nervous it might get yanked, like *Santa Rosa*, the last one she was on.

Even though it's late, I call Billy because I know he'll be up. Back in college, he lived off campus in his own sweet bachelor pad, where we would lounge around on pillows smoking hash out of hookahs and psychoanalyzing each other into the wee hours. "Hello, gorgeous," he says.

"You flatter me so."

"If I don't do it, who will?"

"You got that right, mister."

"You're coming on Sunday night, right? Because just between you and me, I pretty much planned this party for you."

"To what do I owe the honor—or, should I say, pressure?"

"Call it what you want, but your future husband awaits an introduction."

Billy has never set me up with anyone before, so this comes as a shock. "You're going to introduce me to someone?"

"Yes. Your future husband." He sounds pretty confident.

"He's not gay, is he?"

"Okay, I'm going to pretend you didn't say that."

"Sorry, Billy. I just didn't think you knew that many straight guys."

"I know you, don't I?"

"What the hell's that supposed to mean?"

"You're straight."

"Don't jump to conclusions."

"Ooh, you little minx." Billy says, chuckling.

"Don't think I haven't thought about it."

"Good attitude. Listen, he's an old family friend who works with me, and he also happens to be hot, hot, hot."

"You tried to hit on him, didn't you?"

"I will not condescend to answer that question," he says. "You know I'd never set you up with anyone I wouldn't sleep with myself."

"Give me the lowdown," I say, feigning boredom, because unfortunately, I'm starting to feel a little too excited about there being a man, any man, on my horizon. I've had a very dry year.

"Stats? Six two, which I think is the perfect height for—what are you, five ten, five eleven?"

"Five nine. I hope you haven't raised this guy's expectations."

"I don't push what I can't sell, honey."

Now he's spreading it on thick, and I have to say, after the night I've had, it feels pretty good. But I never seem to be able to take a compliment lying down. I always have to interject something like "Yeah, this huge zit on my chin is really something special." Or what I say next, which is "Have you gotten a look at my ass lately?"

"Oh, give it a rest, would you? Your ass is perfect, and believe me, when it comes to asses, I'm an expert. Men, women, dogs . . . I don't want to hear another word about it, okay?"

"I'm serious. I've gained like ten pounds in the last two weeks."

"Well, chill out on the ice cream and go for a run. Look, I saw you three days ago and you looked fine."

"Fine?"

"You looked *maaavelous*. Can I continue please?"

"I'm not so sure this is the best time for me to be meeting someone. I'm not exactly at the top of my game. You know that whole 'you can't be happy with someone else until you're happy with yourself'?"

"It's crap. What you need is to get laid. Then you *will* be happy with yourself and hopefully pass on your appreciation to Mr. Dick Davenport."

"You're shitting me," I say, laughing. "His name is *not* Dick."

"The name his momma gave him."

I'm not sure I buy this "all you need is a good lay" business. It can get your mind off things in the short run, but in the long run, it usually means preoccupation, obsession, and last but not least, crushing heartbreak. To tell the truth, I haven't had sex in so long, I'm not sure I remember how. God knows I don't want anyone getting an eyeful of me naked right now. But I'm an optimist at heart, or maybe a glutton for punishment and can't resist. "Go on."

"He's got dark brown hair and blue eyes the size of saucers."

"That's an attractive visual. He sounds like Bambi," I say, heading for the dusty bottle of Courvoisier in the cabinet underneath the kitchen sink.

"You know what I mean. He's big into skiing, mountain biking, kayaking, ah-*hem*, all of that clean fun you're into—plus, he graduated from Harvard undergrad, MBA Co-lum-bia."

My last two boyfriends barely graduated from high school. My stomach is beginning to knot. Lately, I get completely weak in the knees at the mention of available men. I pour myself a snifter, light up a cigarette, and blow out the smoke.

"Are you smoking?"

"No," I lie. "So he's a suit."

"With a love of the outdoors!"

"A suit with a cause?"

"I guess you could say that."

"What time Sunday?"

○ ○ ○

Saturday is definitely a better day. The first good thing that happens is Jamie boils enough water for the two of us. I'm feeling good, optimistic, even though my groin's still killing me. I swear that flabby winter layer isn't jiggling as much. I'm not sure what this whole body-perception thing is all about. How is it that one day you can feel like a hippopotamus and the very next be puckering up to the mirror? It doesn't make any sense.

The next good thing that happens is I don't get hit by a cab on my way to work, which is a major bonus.

The pinnacle? Walking into the kitchen to find Danny O'Shaughnessy conspicuously absent. Pablo and Javier haven't seen him. My heart jumps. I'm flying. Clearly, Noel's seen through him and canned his ass. Maybe this is going to be my big break? Maybe I'm on sauté tonight!

I pull out a roasting tin, and despite the soreness in my groin, I've got some pep in my step as I head out of the kitchen through the dining room and down to the basement walk-ins to get my vegetables. Ray, the butcher, gives me a smile. He's a good guy, Ray, knows I want to learn all I can about butchering, and takes me aside whenever he's not too busy to show me the proper way of filleting a side of beef or butterflying a leg of lamb. The most important thing is a sharp knife, and Ray has both stone and steel on hand for constant sharpening during operations. "You wanna check out this pork rib?" he asks as I walk by.

"No time," I say, not breaking my stride.

"Hey! Watch out for the shit!"

I stop in my tracks and look down. I'm straddling a dark stream of sludge and water running down the center of the cracked concrete floor. The smell of sewage is strong. "What the hell happened here?" I ask.

"Busted pipe!" Ray calls.

"Beautiful," I mutter and, dodging brown lumps that I hope aren't shit, make my way to the walk-in. Opening the door, who do I see trying to look busy in the corner next to the buttermilk but that bastard O'Shaughnessy. "Danny," I say, hoping he'll leave it at that.

"Hey, Layla, what's shakin'?" he says, slipping something into his pocket.

"Not much," I say, putting down my tray and hunting through boxes for my beets, carrots, and peppers. I don't look at Danny. I want him to get whatever he needs and get the hell out so I can have a quick meltdown. But he's just standing there, staring at the blocks of butter.

"You know what I'm looking for, Layla?"

"No idea."

"The hardest block of butter I can find," he says, wiping his nose a couple of times.

"I'd say all of the butter in here's pretty much the same consistency, Danny."

The beets and carrots are in their usual spot, but someone must have covered the peppers. I'm aggressively looking under cartons of lemons and limes, hoisting and moving things around to give the impression that I'm busier than I am, but Danny keeps on talking. "That's exactly what I've been trying to determine," he says, his voice getting closer.

The walk-in refrigerator is cool, and there are a couple of

dim lights, just enough for you to see what you're doing. Squatting down, my head deep underneath the cold-cut shelf, I can feel Danny standing behind me but pretend not to notice.

"You think you could help me out here?" he asks.

When I turn my head around to look up at him, the tip of my nose brushes against what I'm really hoping isn't—a fat purple hard-on. "So *that's* where the Chinese eggplants are," I say, standing up so that Danny's penis presses against the front of my coat.

"I was sort of hoping you could heat mine up," he says into my ear, putting his arms on either side of my head and locking his hands onto the metal shelving behind me. "You said I could have a taste." His breath smells acrid, like stale beer and something chemical.

"Gee, Danny, I'm flattered," I say, leaning into him before jerking my knee up hard into his balls. This hurts my groin almost as much as it hurts his, and we both scream out in pain.

Danny's bent over groaning when the door swings open and Ray walks in. "Hey, no fair having a party in here without me," he says, clueless, heading for the bucket of parsley and starting to whistle. Danny kneels down and pretends to inspect the lemons. I find the peppers and load them into my tray.

As I'm limping out, trying to look normal, Ray says, "Hey! Can I have some fries with that shake?"

"I need to speak with you," Noel says when I get back to the kitchen. I haven't even started my mise en place yet, but I don't say anything. Noel's the boss. He sits me down, puts his clipboard on the table in front of him, and cocks one eyebrow, a trait that's really started to chap my hide. He says, "I'm sensing a certain amount of tension between us," with disappointment flickering in his eyes.

Tension. That's the understatement of the year. I want to be a wiseass and say something like "Oh, *really?*" But I hold my tongue. I know Noel has called this little meeting because he wants to fire me but is worried I'm going to slap some kind of sexual-discrimination suit on him. The assistant pastry chef is constantly filling out these complaint forms when any of the guys whistle at her or sing their theme song, *"Andale, andale, yo necesito un poquito de chocha caliente."* Translation: "Hurry, hurry, I need a little hot pussy." The last girl who worked the garde-manger brought a suit against the restaurant and won. I'm sure Noel hopes and prays I'll quit. I wait for him to continue.

"Do you know what I'm talking about?"

"I have an idea," I say, pausing again to let him talk. While I'm at it, I begin cataloging his faults—gelled hair thinning on top, the beginnings of what will likely become a massive paunch, puffy, self-satisfied face. He called the meeting, goddammit, he can get to the point.

"I feel like you've been questioning my authority somewhat."

"Well, if becoming frustrated at not being given certain opportunities means I'm questioning your authority, then I guess you have a point."

"You're not ready for sauté."

And here's where you'll see that despite my hard-core veneer, I can be a fragile little flower. I don't scream, "You are so totally out of line, you no-cooking poseur! The only reason you won't put me on the line is because it makes you feel good to be able to deny me something I desperately want!"

Instead, I sit there, stunned. Like, gee, maybe there's a good reason why I'm being discriminated against. This is the way it can go when you're in the thick of things. You can't see the forest for the trees, and you think the guy who's fucking you over might actually have a point. I don't know what to say to him. Does he mean it? Am I really not *ready* for sauté? I know I'm not the greatest cook in the world yet, but surely I deserve a chance. God knows I could do a better job than Danny.

"Is there something wrong with my performance?" I ask, trying to sound diplomatic.

I want details, but all I get is "I do think your performance is suffering a little. I also think it's affecting the dynamic in the kitchen."

Benny comes over and asks if we'd like something to drink. Noel tells him to bring us some water.

I cannot tolerate him blaming me for the downswing in kitchen morale when clearly the problem is O'Shaughnessy. "If anyone is ruining morale," I say, taking a step toward the abyss, "it's the new guy."

Noel's eyes dart from side to side, and his lips tense as though he's trying to decide whether to ring my little neck or slam the table hard. "The *new guy*," he says, leaning forward menacingly, "happens to be an incredibly talented saucier. Unlike you, he's proven himself in some pretty classy establishments, Slim."

I fucking hate it when he calls me Slim. I'd been under the impression that he gave me this nickname both as a compliment and to show what a Steve McQueen–type guy he was. But the tone of his voice makes it sound more like an insult.

"I don't care if he's worked with Jean-Georges! The guy's a coke fiend, a sexual deviant, and, I'm fairly certain, a kleptomaniac!"

"Which brings me to my next question," he says, pressing

his fingertips together and not meeting my eyes. "You don't have any idea what could have happened to Javier's knife?"

"I have some idea," I say, in a tone that indicates everyone has the same idea.

"Because if you give it back right now, I'm willing to overlook the entire incident."

Picture one of those steam-engine pipes with the hole like a mouth going TOOOOOT! I'm completely speechless. Anger is surging up my spine. There's nothing as bad as being blamed for something you didn't do—especially stealing. I never thought I was a violent person, but at this moment I want to beat Noel's face to a bloody pulp. "Are you accusing me?" I say in a voice I'm hoping is as low and even as I'm trying to keep it, "of stealing Javier's knife?"

"I'm not accusing anyone just yet. Not if the knife is returned to my office before the end of service this evening. No one will be there—it can be left anonymously."

"Noel? I'm going to pretend you didn't just accuse me—*me* and not the asshole who clearly took it, who Pablo *saw* sticking it in his box, where you could probably find it right now—"

"I know you don't like Danny."

"Don't like him!"

"I suggest you keep your voice down."

"He tried to stick his dick down my throat in the walk-in ten minutes ago!"

Noel is so taken off guard by this that he involuntarily blurts out "Ha!" before regaining his composure somewhat and continuing, "What happened, you fall asleep in there and wake up with his dick in your mouth? Whoooo, Slim, that's a good one. I knew you needed to get laid, but giving blow jobs in the walk-in, try not to mix work and pleasure, okay?"

When Benny sets the water down in front of us, I'm practically cross-eyed. When I take a sip, the ice shifts quickly in the glass, splashing water all over my face and jacket.

"Watch out for that drinking problem," Noel hoots.

Why the hell do I want to work for this ass wipe, anyway? It's like we're in the middle of a showdown and I am definitely the bumbling guy in white. I'm not breathing right—holding air between breaths for longer than usual—I can feel the pressure building in my head, the vein in my forehead swelling. My nose is running, and after I wipe it with my finger, I realize it's bleeding.

"Hey, Slim, looks like your nose is bleeding," Noel says, giggling like a little kid and chucking a linen napkin across the table.

Catching the napkin just before it lands on my face, I stick the corner of it up my nose and say, "For the record, I did not steal Javier's knife. I'm not a klepto. And I'm not going to quit. You're going to have to fire me and deal with unemployment, and possibly"—and I can't believe I'm actually saying this—"a lawsuit." The blood's coming out pretty hard, because the napkin is half red, and Noel's not laughing anymore.

"I think you should tilt your head back. Benny! Bring some ice over here!"

By now the entire kitchen is looking at us through the pickup window. Before Benny can make it back to the table, Dina's there with a ball of ice wrapped in a towel. "Excuse us, Chef," she says, looking like she's about to throttle him.

"Well, if it isn't Florence Nightingale. I'll leave you to minister," he says, slowly picking up his clipboard and heading toward the kitchen. "Hey, Layla! When the blood stops, get crackin' in here, we've got a five-thirty on the books!"

Dina walks me over to one of the banquettes and lays me down. Putting one hand under my neck to make tilting it more comfortable, she uses the other to hold my hand over the towel of ice. She's dressed for her shift in a low-cut halter top that ends just above her tattooed navel and low-rider jeans. Her bangles are resting against the side of my chin. "I think you should quit," she says.

"No, that's what he wants me to do."

"You know, some jobs aren't worth making a point for. I heard the whole thing. He's just trying to get your hackles up. Is this the way you want to spend your days? With some cock-sucker trying to get you to quit? And that fucking new guy. Did I hear you say something about him sticking his dick in your face? You should call the police and file a report."

"It's not my style."

Dina takes the ice off my nose to check if it's still bleeding. When she tilts my head forward, thick red blood pours down. "Fuck, this isn't stopping. If it doesn't stop in like five more minutes, I'm calling an ambulance."

"No! I've got to get back in there. It'll be fine," I say, trying to sit up. "I'm dizzy."

"Yeah, no kidding. You're losing a lot of blood."

"Don't call an ambulance, I'll take a cab."

"You're not going by yourself. I think you may have popped a blood vessel or something."

"Maybe Noel will take me," I crack.

"Is there anyone I can call?"

"Gustav? I can't remember if tonight's his night off."

"Don't move. I'm going over to Perla."

Benny takes Dina's spot, and she says, "Do not let her move."

"Right, boss."

Within minutes, Gustav is bending over me in the banquette. By this time I'm on my third towel, and there's blood all over the front of my white jacket. "Chaysus!" Gustav says. And then to Dina, "How long has she been bleeding like this?"

"I think it started around fifteen minutes ago."

Their voices become a din. I can't focus on what they're saying anymore. Gustav presses the linen napkin hard against my nostrils, and I gulp blood down the back of my throat. My head is all fuzzy. I feel my legs dangling and I'm gone.

I wake up in the emergency room at New York–Presbyterian to find a doctor sticking a long metal object up my nose. "Hello," he says, "you lost consciousness for a moment or two."

"More like half an hour, Doc." Gustav is sitting in a chair beside the bed, looking concerned. I'm still in my bloody jacket and checked pants, but my clogs and socks are off. "How you feeling, babe?"

Lying here pathetically covered in dried blood, I'm suddenly overcome that someone cares how I feel. Tears well up, and before I know it, I'm bawling. The doctor, who looks a little too young to know what he's doing, says, "Hey, hey, settle down. We just cauterized that. You don't want to open it back up again. These things can be aggravated by stress. In fact, given the absence of trauma, I'd say tension-induced pressure in the head is probably what caused this bloody nose in the first place. Just breathe deeply and try to stay calm."

I nod. Gustav pulls the chair up close to the bed and puts his hand on mine. "Yah, settle down, you little crybaby-eh."

This gets me laughing.

"You look ravishing," Gustav says.

Mustering strength in my right hand, I weakly give him the finger.

○ ○ ○

I'm lying on the couch, drinking a glass of Pinot Grigio, smoking a cigarette, and watching *The Daily Show with Jon Stewart* when Jamie comes in. "Layla? Sweetie? Where are you? My God," she says, putting down her Kate Spade handbag and placing her keys on the glass coffee table. "Tell me."

So I tell her, "I had a bad day."

"He-*yeeah*," she says, like a Valley girl, "I'd say. But what happened? I stopped by Tacoma tonight, and they told me you'd been rushed to the hospital."

"Well, first this psychopath stuck his dick in my face."

Holding up her hand, she says, "Stop. What? Someone stuck his doodle in your face?"

"It looked like a Chinese eggplant."

"They really can be so unattractive."

"Especially when they're attached to scumbags like Danny O'Shaughnessy."

"But he didn't hurt you, right? He's not the reason you had to go to the emergency room?"

"Indirectly."

It's tiring, but she listens without interruption while I explain the whole deal. And, to my amazement, she seems to relate.

Julia calls at nine to remind me to watch *Intrigues*. I decide not to tell her about my day, and she doesn't ask.

"Puppy, I really think this is going to be my big break. The director is a wonderful man—extremely pleased with my work. Everyone's working incredibly well together, and did I tell you? I bought a new Mercedes convertible? Maybe it's not smart to blow all of my money, but I figured hey, I deserve it, right? Maybe I'll take it out to Nantucket this summer and you can ride in it? Paolo and I are going to Belize at the end of the month, I can hardly wait. We'll be staying at that jungle resort. Remember the one I told you I read about in *Travel and Leisure?* The one owned by Francis Ford Coppola?"

I want to hang up. Who needs a *jungle* vacation right now? The high-paid nighttime soap star and her Italian boy toy? Or me, the burnt-out vinaigrette maker whose career is going down the tubes, is freaked about finances, and hasn't been laid in a year?

When Julia's on the line, I can put the phone down for whole minutes and pick up again pretty much where I left off. I would like to take that Mercedes for a spin, though. Fat chance. She'll have to get bored with it first.

"Well, you know, I told them I'd been riding horses since you were a little girl, so they agreed to let me do my own riding in the scene. Oh, puppy, wait till you see me—bareback, on the beach . . ."

They must be trying to cultivate some sort of middle-aged love story, because the thought of my mother riding a horse bareback on the beach is really too much. Not that she can't pull it off. One of the dubious benefits of being the product of a shotgun wedding is having a mother who looks young enough to be my sister. She's an attractive forty-eight-year-old woman, so I guess they wouldn't have had her do it if she wasn't convincing.

When the time of her show draws near, she wants to stay on the phone so she can talk me through it, give me the heads-up on the subtler nuances of camera angles and lighting. But I tell her I'll be able to appreciate her performance more if I can (prevent myself from slitting my wrists and) give it my undivided attention.

Before she gets off, she asks me her two-pack question— "Any news on the love front?" and "Are you a chef yet?" Which I know she doesn't care nearly as much about as the first.

Then she says, almost as an afterthought, "By the way, I'll see you on Sunday night. Billy is such a sweetheart, always including me in things."

I'm going to kill Billy. I know he likes having Julia around so that he and his gay buddies can belt out show tunes with her at the piano, but I thought this party was my vehicle. Not that I'm optimistic. I'm not much good at being set up with people, and I have to wonder whether Billy is capable of selecting a guy I'll be attracted to.

I don't know what it is about guys in this city, but I have not been impressed with the pickings. I tend to go for the unavailable types, the ones who are amazingly enthusiastic at the beginning but slowly find themselves up to their ears in work. Even if they're unemployed. I'm looking to change my type, though. No more hard-drinking, dirty Lower East Side boys for me. I want a guy I can depend on, be friends with, go for bike rides with. I can't take any more dead-end obsessions. One more of those might kill me. Is it too much to want to love someone and be loved in return? Why does saying that make me want to smack myself? At the first sign of unavailability, I will walk this time, I swear.

When I get off the phone, I begin channel-surfing. I'm not sure I feel like watching *Intrigues*. There might be something better on. But it's Friday night, so probably not. The phone rings, and I let the machine answer while I help myself to another glass of Pinot Grigio. It's Billy, so I pick up. "You are so up shit creek, my friend."

"Is that any way to greet the man who's going to introduce you to Prince Charming?"

"You know what, Billy? You're not going to dangle the carrot after putting on cleats and walking all over me."

"You've really gotta give that metaphor thing a rest."

"You know what I'm talking about," I say, taking a slug of wine and lighting another cigarette.

"I swear I don't." He sounds genuinely perplexed.

"Does the name *Julia* ring a bell?"

"Oops . . . Look, I thought it would be a nice gesture. I haven't seen The Julia since graduation."

"Yeah, she barely made it."

"Look, I didn't think she'd accept. But I have to say, there are going to be a lot of happy queens at that party."

"Sounds like the perfect environment for falling in love."

"Come on, it'll be fun."

"I don't think I'm coming."

"Don't you dare—"

". . ."

"Don't be such a goddamned baby. She's your mother, for God's sake, can't you try to enjoy her every once in a while?"

"I'm not in the mood."

"Well, you better get in the mood, Miss Thang. I'm having this party catered by Taste, and I've already ordered four cases of Veuve."

This is just like Billy. Trying to make me believe that the party's for my benefit when he's probably been planning it for months and has his own potential conquests lined up. "I'm sure Julia will appreciate it," I say, and hang up.

I feel badly enough about hanging up on him that when the phone starts ringing ten seconds later, I pick it up to apologize. "Billy?" There is heavy breathing on the line. "Hello? Anybody there?"

More throaty breathing, getting faster. "You want to make me hot? Huh?"

I don't believe this. I didn't think this sort of thing ever really happened, and today of all days I get the call. Some horny jerk thinking he can use me for his masturbatory pleasure. "ARE YOU WHACKING OFF RIGHT NOW?" I say loudly, practically screaming.

The heavy breathing stops, and there's silence on the other end of the line.

"ARE YOU?"

I hear a quiet "No."

"How old are you?" I demand.

Click.

I'm wearing a see-through white tank top and a pair of boxers. There's a black-and-blue mark the size of a small dog on the side of my thigh. Looking out toward the windows across the way, I try to spot if someone's got a telescope aimed at me. Nothing. I hardly ever draw the curtains. I figure if I get a kick out of looking at other people in their private spaces, why should I deny them the pleasure of watching me lie here like a battered housewife, watching TV and getting drunk on cheap wine? It might help them feel less alone.

I call Billy back and say, "I'm sorry."

He says, "You should be."

"I just got one of those heavy-breather calls."

"You diiiiid?" he says, sounding a little too enthusiastic.

"Yes, I did. Do you think I should be scared?" Because as tough as I like to think I am, this kind of thing does freak me out.

"You? Queen of the asskickers? Go and get one of your knives. Oh, wait, what about that meat cleaver you showed me? No one will fuck with you if you start waving that thing around."

When I get off the phone with Billy, I get up and hobble to the door, where my knife case is propped next to the umbrellas, underneath the coat rack. Clutching the heavy meat cleaver to my chest, I go back to the sofa and watch the opening credits of Intrigues. There are horses, lots of them—running together in the improbably green southern California countryside. They shot seven episodes of Intrigues outside L.A., and they won't shoot any more until they know whether it sinks or swims. This is what enables Julia to hang way too close to me in Manhattan, gathered around the TV with friends, giving everyone the blow-by-blow of each scene she's in. I've sat there with her entourage—most of them men, many of them gay—forcing oohs and aahs convincingly, as though they're watching something quality, like Gone With the Wind or Apocalypse Now, instead of some Dynasty rip-off. But Julia needs that kind of ass kissing. She's beautiful and moderately talented. She knows it and yet she doesn't, if you know what I mean.

Part Dr. Quinn Medicine Woman, part Linda Evans (if you can picture it), my mother, Julia Mitchner, clutches a golden palomino with her skinny, muscular legs. Her bleached-blond hair is long, her shirt a gauzy white, her jeans worn to give that cool, lived-in look—just loose enough. I've got to hand it to her, the woman can ride. She gets paid big bucks to spend her days galloping around the California desert on Hollywood horses, while I make a hundred a day chopping parsley in a kitchen with no windows. I'm so jealous, I can barely stand to watch. It's beautiful though—she's clearly the only one in the cast who knows how to ride, and they play it up, showing her on a horse in practically every other shot.

Her TV husband, an old-timer from *Days of Our Lives*, looks a little like David Hasselhoff. He's attractive, rich, and conniving. Julia is sincere, sexy, and long-suffering. They have TV children who, in reality, are practically their parents' age, getting into all sorts of interracial and bisexual mischief.

The phone starts ringing again. I don't want to pick it up, lest it's the breather. I let the machine get it. It's Julia. "Puppy? Puppy, are you there? I really hope you're *somewhere* watching my show. Look, do me a favor. I've made up these cards—you know—for the show, with the date and time and everything. Very tasteful. I want to send you some so you can give them to your friends at the restaurant, okay? I know you don't have a doorman"—beeeep!

What am I now, a bus shelter? You know that card is going to be a full-on close-up glossy of hers truly. Sometimes I really feel like killing myself. She knows I'm struggling to pay my rent while she drives around in a brand-new Mercedes convertible. And now she wants me to help promote her show? The sad thing is, I'll probably do it.

Running my hand along the sharp edge of the cleaver, I think of disappearing into the night, never to be heard from again. I could move to Fiji or Bombay. I've got three pints of

Ben & Jerry's working in the freezer—Coffee Heath Bar Crunch, Mint Chocolate Cookie, and Chubby Hubby. They have become my best friends.

Muting Intrigues, I get up and walk to the kitchen. I'm glassy-eyed, excited. I can think of nothing but the cool, sweet, creamy relief I'm about to experience. Moving quickly, I take out all three containers and scoop two spoonfuls from each into a coffee mug. Hobbling back to the sofa, I take small bites to make it all last longer, chewing slowly on crunchy, sweet-salty bits of pretzel laced with peanut butter, mint chocolate cookie, toffee bars. The sugar surges through my body, the cream making me feel like a babe suckling at my mother's breast (a sensation I've had to re-create for myself based strictly on fantasy). God, sweet relief! As I stare at the screen, there's a close-up of Julia, looking wistfully at the mountains from the veranda of her enormous mansion. Husband Edgar has just zoomed off in his Porsche Boxster.

Sunday morning I wake up feeling full and disgusted with myself. Unfortunately, this is always the time I choose to scrutinize myself naked. It's hard enough to keep from eating at work. But even away from the kitchen these days, I seem to need food just to feel okay. My body in general has potential. The breasts are a little on the small side, but after the age of eighteen, I started to see this as a good thing. From the front, and standing up, everything looks fine. Slouched on the toilet, though, two pinchable rolls squeeze into each other. Tiny ripples have somehow gathered on my inner thighs, and catching sight of my ass in the bathroom light (I've brought a chair in and am standing on it to get the Full Monty) is like seeing

Freddy's horrifying face pop out of the shadows in *Nightmare on Elm Street*. Disgusting myself further, I scrunch my butt cheeks for the full effect, pressing my fingers up and down the back of my thighs to gauge the damage—which is pretty fucking severe, all the way from my outer thighs to the squishy mass that is my ass. Scrunching, jiggling, jumping up and down—by the time I'm through, I never want to take my clothes off again. It's the ice cream, why can't I just stop eating it? What's my problem? I am a weak, weak human being. Julia has always told me I don't have any discipline, that I get by on minimal effort. And at this stage, I'm starting to agree with her. I am a fucking dilettante. I should feel lucky someone's willing to pay me to toss salads.

o o o

"Everyone!" Billy claps after kissing me on both cheeks and putting my flowers in a vase. A roomful of men with a smattering of assorted women I don't know turn from their conversations. "The maiden of honor, Layla Mitchner." Nods, smiles.

Billy's apartment is impeccable in the manner of an Upper East Side matron's, even though he lives on the Upper West Side. Luxurious striped curtains, swept back with thick golden rope from eight floor-to-ceiling windows, match the love seats by the fireplace. Oil paintings of hunting scenes are strategically positioned along the walls.

Billy could afford to live in this style with or without his editorial position at *Divas*. His father made millions in the garment business before marrying the heiress to the Reynolds fortune. Billy gets more dividend money each quarter than most upwardly mobile couples clear in two years. He is dressed in casual, expensive charcoal-gray slacks and a violet Brooks Brothers oxford that complements his chestnut hair and freckles. I'm wearing the usual—Levi's, a Gap turtleneck, and a pair of low-heeled chocolate-colored suede ankle boots. "Didn't I tell you to wear something sexy? A skirt, perhaps? A nice little top? Sport some toe cleavage?" Billy's talking into my ear. "It wouldn't kill you every once in a while, you know."

I've explained this to him a hundred times. I don't feel comfortable walking the streets of Manhattan in a skirt or dress and high or even low heels. I've got to be able to run like hell if I need to, and I don't like people staring at my legs on the subway. He's lucky I made an effort with the boots. My stomach is churning. I've scanned the room—some of the guys are attractive, but then, most of them are gay. One of them in particular, tall, dark, and handsome, is following two steps behind Billy looking ready to fall to his knees as soon as he gets the signal.

"Who's the god?" I ask Billy.

"I've got one word for you," he whispers in my ear. "Brazilian."

We're in the chef's kitchen now, and Billy's reaching into the customized glass-doored wine chiller. There are bottles of Veuve stacked six high and two deep. The caterer looks like he's about to have a heart attack. His face is red, greasy brown frizzed hair pulled back in a tiny ponytail, forehead dripping sweat. He's checking on something in the oven. There's a large snifter of something amber on ice on the counter near the fridge.

Billy squeezes two crystal champagne flutes into the mess on the granite island in the middle of the kitchen. He has a linen napkin over the cork and slowly eases it out of the bottle. "And," a soft pop, "perfect." He fills our glasses, puts a bubble preserver on the bottle, and slips it into a silver bucket filled with ice. "To you, darling."

"Sometimes I really wish you weren't gay," I say before tilting my head back and letting the cold, crisp bubbles float down my gullet.

"Oyster?"

"You've got oysters?"

Billy gives me a wink and says, "You bet I do. Martin? Where are the oysters? For that matter, where's the ice bar?"

Sweating Martin looks up from where he's hunched over the oven. The emanating aromas smell carcinogenic. "The oysters are in the fridge. My guy was supposed to be here an hour ago. I've been trying to reach him."

"Your guy? What guy? How much am I paying you again? I thought there were supposed to be three other people working here. Where is he?"

Martin is dressed in chef's whites, a soggy paper toque perched precariously on his head. One walleye is looking off to the side, the other opens wide before Martin asks, "You don't mind if I make a long-distance call, do you?"

Billy's going to lose it. "Long-distance call? For what?"

"The oyster guy lives out in Connecticut."

"Oh, for fuck's sake, go ahead." Then, looking at me, Billy says, "Let's get the hell out of here. We've got more important things on the agenda for tonight."

"Are you sure? I can fill in if you want. I know how to shuck."

"I would rather eat maggots than have you work this party. Follow me."

"Is he here?"

"Over by the fireplace, talking to Lucinda. Have you met Lucinda? The beauty editor?"

My heart pounding, I try to suss out the situation on Dick Davenport before making his acquaintance. Looks okay from a distance—tall, dark hair, sport coat—a bit of a prepster . . . Lucinda, spindly legs sticking out from her micromini, looks like a strawless scarecrow. "Does she eat?"

"Hmm. Not sure about that. It's really not very attractive, is it?"

"Obviously some people like it," I say, taking a large gulp of champagne.

"Don't tell me you're jealous."

I give him a look. He knows I don't get jealous of women who look sick. It's the ones with great muscle tone and minuscule amounts of cellulite (a woman's got to have a little bit of meat on her) I envy.

As we approach, Dick Davenport looks up and smiles. Nice smile, straight teeth, nose on the crooked side, but what the hell. The shoes—loafers with tassels. Oh my God. I cannot stand those shoes. Only weenies wear shoes like that. *Layla, stay open, be positive.*

Lucinda won't even look at me—it's like I'm not standing there—until Billy says, "Lucinda, I'd like you to meet Layla. Dick, Layla."

"Nice to meet you," Dick says, shaking my hand. *Warm, dry— let me get a look at those hands—nice nails, good shape, decent size.*

Lucinda gives a terse smile and drops her head ever so slightly in acknowledgment.

Who is she, Queen Elizabeth? I cannot stand coy, bitchy women and like to call attention to their coy bitchiness whenever I can. So, super friendly, I thrust out my hand and cheerfully say, "Hey, Lucinda, nice to meet you! Loved the spread in the February issue."

I firmly clasp her cold, sweaty, limp hand in mine and shake it a couple of times. "Excuse me," she says, extracting her hand like I'm a leper. "I need a refill."

"I'll go with you," Billy says, the two of them walking off together.

Subtle.

Dick, Dick, Dick. Why tassels? Why?

"Glad you read the magazine," Dick says, smiling.

"Oh, I didn't really read it," I say, taking a small sip of champagne. The minute I see Dick's face change, I know I've blown it, so I say, "The February issue, that is."

"I'll send you a copy."

"Thanks," I say, demurely sipping my champagne. What I could really use is some Valium, something to take the edge off, make me care less what some Dick Davenport thinks of me. I'm uncomfortable. Very. And why? Because this moderately handsome guy with tassels on his shoes is single?

"So what do you do?" Dick asks. *Original.*

"I'm a cook."

"Really? You're a chef?" This is a common response from people who have never worked in a restaurant.

"No, I'm a cook. There's a difference." *How many times have I given this speech?* "The chef is the chief, the guy who runs the show, the one in charge. I'm just a plebe."

"So what do you cook?"

"At the moment, not much. I'm a salad specialist."

Dick laughs. "A salad specialist, huh?"

"It's more like architecture or masonry than cooking. Constructing lettuce edifices that jut from the plate and stay that way from kitchen to customer."

"Sounds rough." He takes a sip from his champagne glass. There is a painful lull. He looks uncomfortably down at his shoes.

He thinks I'm a loser. And why shouldn't he? I think I'm a loser. I'm sweating. This isn't easy. Conversation is not flowing. I should have run the other way when I saw the tassels. But I was optimistic, I had hope. "What do you do?" I ask.

"I guess you could say I'm a businessman," he says, looking bored.

"You work with Billy, right?"

Dick smiles and says, "Yeah, you could say that."

"Are you in marketing?"

"Um, no." To his credit, he looks sort of embarrassed when he says, "I own *Divas* and a few other magazines and cable channels."

Dick Davenport. "Are you related to the Davenports of Davenport Corp.?"

"That would be me."

"Wow." *Nothing like struggling into the family business.* "So you work for your father?"

"Some people would say *he* works for *me*."

"Does modesty run in the family?" I ask, unable to control myself.

Dick gives me an icy stare before saying, "No, it doesn't." Then, straightening his tie in what looks like an effort to compose himself and salvage some decent conversation, he says, "Tell me, what's the inside scoop on good places to eat?"

"That depends on what you like." *Silver spoons in your mouth? Having your cake and eating it too?*

"Something authentic, it doesn't matter what, as long as it's true to what it's supposed to be."

"You have good culinary insight for a businessman."

"Well, when you're brought up with a French kitchen staff, it's kind of hard not to have," he says, staring at me hard. He's not smiling, and I can't tell what that look is on his face. Is he jerking my chain? Is my bitterness that palpable?

Ever since *my* daddy kicked me out of my cozy nest, you see, I've had little interest in people who don't have to struggle—do things the hard way. I want stories of losing it all, friends and family deriding those who dare to dream, working three crappy jobs just to afford a morsel of food . . . I want tales of suffering! I'm still waiting to experience the self-confidence and sense of accomplishment my father promised would be mine. Until then, snooty little rich kids like the boy Davenport will continue to bug the shit out of me.

Draining my champagne, I decide there's no place I could mention that he hasn't already been. Besides, I don't like revealing my secret jewels to dorks like Dick. I'm relieved when I hear "Everyone?" It's Billy with the introductions, and it's starting to feel like a formal ball at Versailles. "The lovely, the incomparable, the talented"—everyone's smiling and going along, even Julia, who stands there in all her glory, gracefully accepting her praise—"Julia Mitchner!"

There is applause, a tinkling of crystal. Clad in an expensive burgundy silk top, fitted leather pants, and ankle-breaking high-heeled pointy boots, Julia looks like winter hasn't touched her. It's January and she's sporting a late-August tan, which accentuates her hair's golden hue.

"You related?" Dick asks in a tone that expects a no.

"Mmm," I say.

"Sisters?"

"No, she's my mother."

"You're Julia Mitchner's daughter? I didn't know she had a daughter," he says, as if I'm lying.

"She doesn't like to play me up." I notice him looking dubiously at my hair, then over at Julia's. "We're both naturally brunette," I explain, "although she hasn't been since around the time of my birth." I need another drink, and no one's coming forth with the refills. "Can I get you some more champagne?" I ask, hoping on some level to shame him. Making sure a lady's glass is never empty is the sort of task guys like Dick are primed for since birth.

"I'm sorry. Please, let me," he says, turning abruptly and walking off toward Billy and Julia, presumably a pit stop on his way to the kitchen.

He's probably going over there to check out my story. Dick.

I pretend to take a curatorial interest in Billy's oil paintings. Everyone else is engrossed in conversation while the fat-assed spinster inspects the artwork. It's that moment in the evening when you feel like you're falling down the rabbit hole, and if something doesn't change fast, you're likely to crack completely. What was I thinking? Billy setting me up. HA!

Refusing to look in her direction can't stop Julia's laughter from grating on my inner ear, seeping into my brain and down, down into where I can feel it puckering my sphincter. Dick Davenport is not coming back with the champagne, so I head for the kitchen. On my way in, I hear a chorus of "I'm starved"s and "Wasn't there supposed to be food at this party?" The only food items I've seen so far are the assorted bowls of nuts and olives on the antique side tables.

A low, urgent, drunk voice is saying, "Hoddmanit, Dan, Dan, dondodistome. You can't tellmedat now, not tonight. We'll talkaboudid layder. No! No, YOU WILL NOT move out tonight. Please." Looking up at me, Martin cups his hand around the mouthpiece, leans against the blond wood frame of the kitchen door and changes tack. "The party's in full swing, and I'm loosinit, man. The petits fours are burnt to a fuckin' crisp, the crostinis r'toast and d'tapenade's f'shit. S'like shoe polish. Oysters! Fuckin' fuck the oysters, I'm not shuckin' all those fuckers myself! You'reda mastashucker, sershiously, no one shucks like you, ha, ha, ha!" Martin's giggling desperately, like it's just occurred to him that whoever this person is—his lover and business partner, no doubt—will never shuck with him again. "I don't even know how to shuck!"

Tapping Martin on the shoulder, I mouth, "I'll help you."

"Hold on a minute." He cups his hand over the phone and looks up at me. I can see tears welling in the corners of his eyes. "What? Hand me a tissue."

Grabbing the tissue box off the counter, I pull one out and hand it to him. I say, "I'm a cook. I know how to shuck."

"Fridge," he says, before turning back to his crumbling life.

I cover three silver trays with crushed ice. The oysters are in bags that look like nets. I pull a kitchen towel off the handle of the refrigerator and select a short knife with a thick handle from the assortment in Billy's knife rack. Of course Billy would have the perfect knife for shucking oysters, even though I'm sure he's never used it. It looks brand-new. Billy never cooks.

Bobby Flay taught me the secret trick to shucking at a party at Bruce and Eric Bromberg's house out in East Hampton. They're all huge now, Bruce and Eric with Blue Ribbon et al.

and Bobby with Mesa Grill et al., new cookbooks, and a television show. They put me to work at the enormous four-sided grill they'd set up in the backyard next to the roasting pit where a cuchinillo (young suckling pig) was being basted on a spit, turning darker shades of pink. I had no idea who Bobby was at the time, and the two of us were working side by side, flipping peppers and onions, zucchinis, squash, swordfish steaks, and New York strips. Fresh out of the Cordon Bleu, I thought I was pretty hot shit, ordering Bobby around like a redheaded stepchild. He was very nice about it. Took my guff and told the other grill cooks to listen to the chef. It was the best cooking time I ever had, feeling like I was one of the guys. When I found out who Bobby Flay was, I was mortified. And then I thought, *Wow, he was so cool. He never once pulled rank or made me feel like I didn't know what I was doing. He let me be in control.* I guess that's what happens when you're the real McCoy. You don't need to piss on other people to make yourself feel better.

The trick to shucking is twisting the edge of your knife into the back hinge of the oyster to loosen it up, then quickly moving the tip to the side and wrenching it open. Easy. After years of trying to poke the tip of the knife into the front crease of the shell and doing nothing but chipping it, I found this method a real eye-opener. People are always impressed by oyster shucking because they think it's hard.

I move on to the second dozen, arranging them neatly in the crushed ice and garnishing with twisted rondelles of lemon. Martin sniffles and pleads in the background, and I can hear Billy's voice approaching. "I will kill her if she's in— Well, look who's here!"

Julia moves toward me in all of her bronzed splendor, fumi-

gating the immediate vicinity with Chanel No. Five. "Puppy!
What are you doing?" After she gives me the *deux bises*, I can see
her eyes onceing me over. Without a trace of subtlety, she says,
"Are you working in pastry now?"

My ears are getting hot.

"Have you been *eating* pastries?" She appears aghast at my
condition.

Granted, I've put on maybe fifteen pounds since the last
time she saw me. I am no longer a fighting 125 but a softer 140.
Gripping the short, thick-handled shucking knife, I notice my
knuckles are white. I don't want her to know how much she's
hurting me, do not want to respond but can't stop myself. Like
the child I no longer want to be, I ask in a tone I'm afraid be-
trays the depth of my insult, "Do I look fat?"

Shaking her head sadly a couple of times, Julia decides dis-
cretion's in order and gets closer to my ear. "I think we all know
when we're not at our perfect weight, don't we? I can feel an
extra pound like a boulder on my body. I have a wonderful new
trainer, but I'm not sure you could afford him."

"Probably not." I have been in the presence of my mother
for all of five minutes, and already I'm spiraling into depths of
self-loathing I never thought I could sink to.

"I'm not sure that outfit is the most flattering thing either,"
she says, craning her head around to inspect. "Skirts can be
wonderful camouflage."

"Thanks, Julia, I'll keep that in mind."

"You're supposed to be mingling. This is no way for a young
woman to behave at a party with so many available men!" she
says with forced optimism.

This must be the sort of judgment she displayed when agreeing to marry husband number two, the flaming polo player. Even if they weren't all gay, who'd want to mingle with a pastry eater like me?

Then, in lower tones, "Billy told me he has a man here for you. Have you met Dick yet? He's absolutely charming. I want you to put that knife down, clean yourself up, maybe put on a touch of makeup, and come out here. You're missing all the fun! I'm going to sing your favorite just as soon as I refill my champagne. Are those oysters? Let me at 'em," she says, doing her Mae West imitation.

I want her out. No, I want her dead.

I can hear Billy trying to reason with Martin, getting no-where. Moving up close behind me, Billy asks, "How're you coming with those?"

"Only five more dozen to go."

"I feel terrible, Lay. You really shouldn't."

"But I must."

"I can't argue with that. The natives are getting restless." As an afterthought, he says, "So whaddaya think of Dick?"

"You told me you worked *with* him."

"With, for, what's the difference? Is Benicio del Toro stand-ing behind me?"

Looking over his shoulder, I can see Miguel, white teeth flashing, brown eyes heavy-lidded and misty. "How come you get all the babes? Here," I say, pushing a tray of oysters into his hands. "Take this out and come back in five minutes for an-other."

"Puppy, puppy, promise me you'll come out and listen as soon as you're done, would you? I won't sing 'New York, New York' until then," Julia says, winking at me before dramatically turning, her long blond hair swinging, giving the impression of a genie or a mirage before, like a bad dream, she disappears.

Putting down the knife and washing my hands, I walk out onto the balcony of Billy's bedroom, which has a sweeping view of the Hudson, the Palisades, the lights of Midtown and the Upper West Side. Lighting a cigarette, I inhale deeply and blow smoke out into the cold air. My head itches, and I stand there smoking, scratching my scalp, then sniffing my fingers. I need a haircut.

When I go back in the kitchen, Dick Davenport is in the champagne cooler, pulling out a fresh bottle of Veuve. Ignoring him, I scrub my hands at the sink, pick up a towel, and start back in on the oysters.

"Hey, you're pretty good at that. You must be a *cook*," he says, popping the cork. "I never did get you that refill, did I?"

"Nope," I say, shrugging and breathing out in mock disappointment. "And now it's too late, because I don't drink when I'm working."

"I thought all cooks drank while they worked."

"Yeah, and all business guys get hammered at lunch."

"I myself am quite fond of the three-martini lunch," he says sarcastically. "Can I get you something else? Some Pelegrino or something?"

"No thanks." I start shucking faster, and soon I realize I'm showing off.

Dick watches in silence, sipping his champagne. "You do that very well," he says.

"Thank you," I say, focusing hard, lest I slip and bury the knife in my palm.

"Where do you work, anyway?"

"Tacoma."

"I've heard good things."

"The food's not bad."

"Maybe I'll stop by sometime."

"Maybe you should."

"Well, I think I'll be heading back in, if you don't mind."

Mind? Why should I mind? I'll just stay in here working my ass off because that's what I do! I work! Unlike certain tassel-loafered champagne sippers who will remain nameless. Now comes the moment when, despite the fact that I'd rather be shucking oysters in the kitchen than socializing with a bunch of snooty media types, I still want people to realize what I'm doing and appreciate me for it. Listening to Martin sob, I start to seethe. The whole evening has become an ugly metaphor for what has become my life. *Just one more dozen and you can get the hell out of here.*

When I head into the living room, Julia's sitting seductively on top of the piano, an effeminate mystery man accompanying her. She's singing "Memory" while everyone listens apprecia-tively, staring at her in awe. She looks incredible. Billy's in a corner whispering sweet nothings to Miguel, and Lucinda's standing next to Dick, looking like the cat that swallowed a ca-nary.

No one notices as I slide out the door.

○ ○ ○

It's Monday, and I'm riding across town in the spitting rain on Eighth Street. I'm headed toward Astor Hair—the "I don't give a shit" hair salon. My hair is long, curly, unruly, and who needs it, working in a kitchen. Besides, I've got to shake up my life a little. Get my mind off the fact that things could not be going less my way.

Locking the bike to a No Parking sign, I walk inside and shake the rain off my waterproof jacket. It's so warm the windows are fogged up, the overhead lights producing a white-gray glow. You don't need an appointment at Astor Hair.

The mostly foreign hairdressers—men and women—sit in chairs looking bored, shooting the shit, or reading magazines, waiting for their victims. Some have people in their chairs whom they stand close to, electric clippers humming. I'm thinking, *It's the East Village, how bad could it be?* I want a cheap haircut, and I've heard you only have to pay twelve bucks here.

I am directed to a chair where a woman with a name tag that says OVID asks me what I want. I hand her a photograph from *Vogue* of an emaciated waif with chickadee-short yellow hair. I think that maybe with this haircut, I will be transformed. "You sure dees whadyou want?" she asks.

I nod.

"Ees vedy short, yes?"

"Yes."

Using a pair of Fiskars, she cuts off around eight inches in less than a minute. Pieces fall to the floor and land on the front of the plastic bib pinned around my neck. There it all goes. My hands are sweaty. I am so excited, nervous, and scared that I can feel my heart palpitating in my chest and smell the wafts of nervous sweat billowing up from my armpits. Ovid keeps brushing her fingers on the side of my neck, and every time she hits a particular tickle spot, a muscle contracts involuntarily and my head tilts, making me look like I've got a twitch.

By the time she sprays my remaining hair with more water (no shampoos here), it's short, up near my ears. Revving up the electric clippers, she sets to it. The more she clips, the more I fear that the *Vogue* picture has not seeped into her artistic hairdressing mind's eye. Our senses of style must be at odds, because what I'm starting to look like is not what I had in mind.

She's given me one of those jobs that's short on the sides and longer on top. I feel like I'm going to cry. Stumbling back out into the rain, I am dazed. Part of me is okay with the fact that I've had all my hair cut off. It feels different, light. I can't stop running my hand up the back and down the sides. I haven't had short hair since that Dorothy Hamill in fifth grade. The other part is sad and angry. Like I've done it to spite myself, make myself even less attractive and more tomboyish than I already am. I have no idea how I really look until I step into the kitchen that afternoon.

Pablo and Javier give me the usual "Hola, como estás, chica?" but don't mention my hair. Joaquin doesn't hold back, though. "Sweetheart, let me give you the number of my hairdresser. You've gotta fix that."

"That bad, huh?" It's what I feared, but sometimes you can't know how sucky things are until you get some outside feedback.

Politely, he says, "No, not bad, exactly." Then, moving in close to whisper in my ear, he asks, "You're not gay, right?"

"No."

"I didn't think so. You don't want to be walking around looking like that, then. You'll have the Cubbyhole brigade sniffing you down. You live in the West Village right near there, don't you?"

I nod. I put the number in my jacket pocket and tie a ban-

danna over the top of my head. All through service, I am obsessed with fixing my hair.

Thankfully, Noel is not as abusive as usual. I had to hear it
from the daytime manager, but apparently he asked Danny if
he could search his big red toolbox. In it, he found Javier's
knife. O'Shaughnessy gave him some lame excuse like "I must
have picked it up out of the dishwasher by accident." I guess
Noel's giving him the benefit of the doubt, because he's
putting together his mise en place, looking oddly ill at ease.

In the end, I decide I am not going to spend good money
after bad. Astor fucked up my hair, they can damn well fix it
again.

The next day, I head back and sit in the chair of a woman
named Olga. She asks, "Who did this to you?" As though she's
just stumbled on me, wounded in a dark glen.

"I don't see the culprit, but I remember her name. Ovid."

"Greek," she says, shaking her head with disgust. "Is short."

"I know."

"If I fix, it will be no more than this long all around." She
holds up her thumb and forefinger, indicating an inch.

I tell her to do what she needs to do to make the top part
shorter, the whole thing more uniform and hopefully more
cool, more fashionable. Afterward, I look nothing like the cool
Vogue waif. More like an unhappy, puffy-faced New Yorker in
the wintertime.

"That's the good thing about hair," she says with a grunt. "It
grows."

o o o

You can whiff that stale-beer smell from a block away. The side-walks in the meatpacking district are slick with the grease of dead meat. In the wintertime, when the fat freezes, it can get downright treacherous.

The Hogs is packed. It didn't used to be this way. Back when it first opened, it was hardly ever crowded. There was even room to dance the two-step in front of the jukebox. It has since been discovered, and cringingly, a red velvet rope barricades a line of people waiting to get inside. Zinc, the three-hundred-pound Harley-riding bouncer, knows me and moves the rope aside while holding back the bridge-and-tunnel.

A bunch of bikers sing "God Bless America" over in one cor-ner. Micky, the bartender, wears tight jeans and a corset and line-dances on top of the bar to "These Boots Are Made for Walkin'." I'm a little late. I want to get drunk. Fast. Dina's al-ready up at the bar, drinking a bottle of Bud. She likes to slum it when she's not working. No fancy top-shelf drinks for her. Putting an arm around me, she kisses my cheek and, in a low, perfumed, beery breath, says, "Check out the hunk at the end of the bar."

A guy with shaggy blond hair, baseball cap, and several days worth of facial hair quietly broods. I can't tell if I think he's a hunk or not. I nod.

"Wanna meet him?"

"Not tonight."

"What's the matter with you? I thought you wanted to have some fun."

"I do. And tonight that doesn't include men. Besides, I'm moving to San Francisco."

"Say what?" She's got her arm cocked, bottle poised to drink, but has stopped midmotion. "Don't do it," she says, shaking her head and taking a swig of her beer. "Shit, he's looking over here. He's looking at you! Don't look, don't look."

"Oh, please. I've been scaring women in ladies' rooms all over this city because they think I'm a guy. Can I have a drink please?" I ask, pulling out a pack of cigarettes.

"Micky!" Dina calls. "A shot of Cuervo and a Bud!"

Micky jumps behind the bar in one athletic movement, and within seconds, I've got a shot of tequila in my hand. Dina already has one sitting in front of her. She picks it up, clinks mine, and we throw them back sans salt and lime.

Dina's thirty-eight years old and has been living with her photographer boyfriend, Stan, for four years. I've seen him at the bar maybe once during my time at Tacoma. I ask her if they're ever going to tie the knot, and she says she never wants to get married. "Why should I ruin everything?" she says. "It's great the way it is."

"But don't you want to have kids?" I ask.

"Not now I don't. Actually, I'm not sure I ever do. Besides, you don't have to be married to have a kid."

"I think I'd like to be married before having a kid."

"So traditional," she says, inspecting her belly tattoo. Then, holding up her beer and clinking her bottle on mine, she emphatically says, "Tradition!"

I don't understand how Dina can be so nonchalant about the kid thing. I ask, "Don't you feel like time's running out?"

Laughing at me, she playfully punches my arm. "What are you worried about? You're still what, twenty-five?"

"Twenty-eight."

"Twenty-eight! Don't worry, Granny, you've still got plenty of time."

"What about you?" I ask.

"Me? I'm not worried. If it happens, it happens. I'm thinking I might freeze an egg or two."

"That sounds romantic."

Just about everyone in the place is smoking. There's a large column next to the bar, and if you shimmy up it and touch the ceiling, Micky of the heaving breast and tiny waist will howl, tell you to tilt your head back, and pour tequila down your gullet.

"About this moving to San Francisco nonsense—what are you thinking?" Dina asks, holding out two fingers to indicate she'd like a cigarette.

"Nothing. It's just a dream I've been having."

"You know I lived there for three years, and you don't see me crying in my beer right now, do you?"

"Wasn't for you?"

"People there are so fucking earnest. Really PC, I'm telling you, it started to mess with me."

"You wanted to kill trees and join the KKK?"

"Ha, ha, ha," she says slowly, unamused.

"I wouldn't mind some mountains and a little bit of fresh air."

"So go to New Paltz!"

"No, I mean *real* mountains. I need to get into shape, feel good about myself. I never should have cut off all my hair. New York City is killing me."

"Micky! Another couple of shots over here!" Dina shouts over the heads of hot young men drinking cans of Pabst Blue Ribbon. "Listen," she says, running her hand along the side of my head, "I think your hair looks really cute."

"You do?"

"Yes, I do," she says unconvincingly. "And I hate to break the news to you, but this city is not what's killing you. You think that just by moving, your life is going to change completely? You're still going to have to deal with dicks like Noel in San Francisco. They'll just be more friendly about it. It's the California way. You also still have to deal with yourself."

All of my daydreaming is extremely rose-colored. I will have a killer job that satisfies me completely, all kinds of free time to go hiking and biking in the nearby mountains, and of course, lots of good-looking mountain boys. It will be nothing like claustrophobic, unnatural old New York with all of its immature little boys and their mindfuck games. It doesn't usually hit me until I've been somewhere new for a while that it's possible to feel shitty in paradise. Funny how this never occurs to me *before*. It's part of what I'm sure Freud might call "the greener grass" complex.

"A Boy Named Sue" is playing on the juke, and Dina says, "You wanna dance?"

Taking a swig of Bud, I say, "Sure."

Two guys standing behind us at the bar step forward and say, "We'll save your seats."

By the time we find a space to dance in, Led Zeppelin's "Over the Hills and Far Away" has started. I love this song. Dina and I dance facing each other in our own world, giving the occasional dreamy smile when we stop rolling our heads around. Dancing is something I don't do enough of these days, and I don't know why. There's the satisfaction of the Jimmy Page air guitar, of singing along with Robert Plant, hitting all the high notes.

We're both sweating as we head back to our seats. The brooder is standing next to mine.

"Holy shit, girl, hot potato twelve o'clock," Dina says, barely moving her lips before looking at him, cracking a glistening, white-toothed smile, then saying, "Hello, handsome."

This is how Dina is. Because she's safe in a relationship with Stan—whom, admittedly, I don't know very well but who seems like a nice enough guy—she can flirt to her heart's content and it never means more than that. Guys, especially New York guys, respond well to this. It's like they can smell that she could give a shit and the confidence that brings. Wanting it (or them) too badly is like wearing skunk perfume.

Against all probability, the brooder looks at me, not at Dina, when he says, "Hi. I'm Frank Stillman."

"Layla Mitchner," I say, and we stare at each other, smiling, before I think to say, "This is Dina."

"Nice to meet you."

"I gotta use the loo," Dina says, jumping up and heading toward the bathroom.

"Very charismatic," Frank says, motioning with his head toward Dina.

"Very," I say, taking a gulp of beer. *Another Dina groupie.*

"What about you?"

"You mean am I charismatic?"

"Well, I can see that by the way you dance."

"I was hoping you weren't expecting me to answer that one." Now that I'm staring right at him, I can see his eyes are clear and interested. He looks sharp, inquisitive, possibly a bit dangerous. The shoe inspection reveals a pair of well-worn black work boots. So far, so good.

"Where you from?" he asks.

"New York, mostly."

"A real New Yorker?"

"Born and bred."

"You're lucky. I love this city."

"You must not be from around these parts, then."

"I grew up in Virginia."

"You don't have an accent."

"Neither do you. I thought all New Yorkers talked like George Costanza."

"Huh. I thought all southerners talked like those guys in *Deliverance*."

"Touché." Frank finishes his beer, tilts up his U.S. Open cap, and asks, "Can I get you another drink?"

"Sure."

Frank has only to stand and look at Micky, and she's popping the tops off two more Buds. "Here ya go, darlin'," she says, giving him a wink. Smiling at her, he looks kind of like Robert Redford in *Butch Cassidy and the Sundance Kid*.

Taking a sip of his beer, he grins at me sideways and asks, "You gonna climb the pole tonight?"

"I don't know," I say. "Are you?"

"I think it's strictly a girl thing," he says, his eyes twinkling.

"I don't know if I'm the type."

"You think you *could* climb the pole?"

"I don't know," I say, giving it serious consideration. "I might need some help." Truth be told, I've monkeyed up that pole more times than I care to count.

Frank clicks his tongue in his cheek and says, "I think it's against the rules." Pausing to give me a cute smile that reveals a couple of sexy dimples, he continues, "I think you need to leave your underwear at the top."

"Hm," I say, smiling back at him, "what if I'm not wearing any?"

"Then I might have to take you to lunch tomorrow."

"That's smooth."

"Yeah, I guess I'm not that smooth," he says, his voice getting quiet, "but I'd still like to take you to lunch."

"I'll think about it." I like this guy. He's cute, engaging, quirky. . . .

After my third shot and fourth beer, apropos of nothing, I blurt, "I used to have long hair!"

Frank says, "I love your hair. It's stylish, sexy. I can't even imagine you with long hair."

Good answer. I don't tell him my short hair would make me feel like a lumberjack if I put on a plaid shirt.

"Both my mother and sister have short hair," he says.

"Is that a good thing?"

"I like them both very much," he says.

Later, during a lull in the conversation, he takes one of my hands in his and says, "Nice." Inspecting them closer, he continues, "Long fingers."

I am self-conscious about the dark oil stains in the crevices of my nails. I tell him I'm a cook and that no matter how hard I scrub them with a coarse brush, I can never get them totally clean.

"And she cooks!" he says, wide-eyed, impressed. Turning my right hand over, he notices the half-moon-shaped birthmark that no one ever notices. "What's this?" he asks.

"A pudding stain."

He looks like he believes me. "Really?"

"No. It's a birthmark."

"You're like a painting," he says, "constantly revealing new things."

I stare at Frank like he can't be serious, and he laughs and says, "What? It's true!"

"The pickup handbook?" I ask.

"You can't take everything in it for gospel, but it's amazingly instructive," he says, running his finger back and forth over the café au lait spot.

Frank has a couple of thick silver rings on his fingers and the nails on his right hand are slightly grown out, "for pickin'," he tells me.

"Not your nose I hope."

"That and my guitar," he says, flicking his pinky nail against the side of his right nostril.

Flannel sleeves over long underwear are pushed halfway up his forearm, which is strong looking, veins pulsing, a tattoo peeking out.

"What's this?" I ask, pointing to the tat.

Pushing his sleeve up further, he says, "Nova Zembla." As I try to make out the archaic block lettering, he says, "It's a fictional kingdom in this book by Nabokov."

"I love *Pale Fire*."

"I love that you love *Pale Fire*," he says.

This guy could be a departure.

Don't ask me why, but this whole Robert De Niro *Cape Fear* thing really gets my motor running. I envision myself walking arm in arm with him through the cobblestoned streets of the meatpacking looking like that Dylan album cover, defining hip.

Out of nowhere he asks, "Do you believe in God?"

"Yes, I do," I reply. "Although the way my career has been going, I'm not sure why. . . ."

"They didn't provide career counseling at Sunday school?"

"That would be Hebrew school."

"With a name like Mitchner?"

"My dad was Scotch Irish but my mother's maiden name was Goldfarb."

"I knew it!" he says, excited. "I don't mind telling you, I've got a thing for Jewish girls."

"We're a screwy bunch," I say.

"Exactly," he says.

Dina has disappeared, and I am grateful. Frank selects two cocktail napkins from the edge of the bar, pulls a pen out of his Carhartt jacket, and begins writing down his information. After handing it to me, he slides the pen and napkin over and says, "Your turn."

As we leave, Frank holds open the door, and Zinc pinches my cheek. Out on the sidewalk there's an icy wind blowing off the Hudson. Frank puts his strong, warmly padded arm around me, and I fit perfectly into the nook. I'm wearing a leather biker jacket and an unflattering gray wool hat that is as fashionable as it is ugly. Frank is maybe six one, six two, and has a loping gait that exudes confidence and sex. He presses himself against me, our legs moving at the same time. His hair is disheveled, his eyes are big and brown, and for reasons I can't fathom, he seems to find me amusing. In short, I am in big fucking trouble.

In the morning, I am alone in my futon on the floor when Jamie pokes her head into my room. "Did I hear a man in here last night?"

"We drank chamomile tea."

Her eyes light up as she sits on the edge of the futon, her

bony knees sticking out from a white Hilton robe pulled tightly
to her chest. "And?"

"Talked."

"Kisses?"

I smile at her. I am euphoric. My stomach is doing cartwheels.

"Good ones?" she asks.

I prop myself up on my arm. I don't want to let on I'm as excited as I am, but I can't help it. "Really good," I say, running
my fingers around the edge of my mouth.

"Stubble?"

"Yeah, a little. Is it red?" I ask, leaning up close so she can inspect.

"Looks like passion," she says, teasing.

The phone rings. Jamie jumps up and runs out of the room.
I can hear her saying, "Just a minute, please," before she
rushes back in holding the receiver against her robe mouthing,
"It's him."

"Hello?" I say as Jamie quietly closes my door.

"I just wanted to call and say good morning."

"Good morning," I say. *I think I'm in love with you.*

"I also wanted to ask when I can see you again."

I feel like the Queen of Sheba. I don't want to seem too enthusiastic, but I want to tell him to come over immediately. I
could make us some coffee, pick up some croissants, and then?

"Sunday's my night off."

"How about I take you out for dinner?"

"Dinner sounds perfect," I say, my heart going ba, ba, ba,
ba, ba, ba! *Rumba.* As I lie back on the futon, the morning light
streams through the window, and I think of the photo that
every college girl used to have in her dorm room of the di-

sheveled white bed bathed in soft slats of sunlight. I have visions of lounging with Frank in this bed, the two of us warm and comfortable in our mutual love. When we're not in bed making passionate love, I'll be in the kitchen baking tart tatin, roasting rosemary-smeared sweet-herb-butter-infused leg of lamb. A glass of champagne? A dollop of crème fraîche? Now come on over here and give me a kiss. . . .

Looking in the mirror, I'm startled to see I have bed head. I can go with it. It looks kind of funky.

It's February and cold, around 28 degrees. I bundle up, head outside, and start to run along the West Side Highway. My groin is still stiff from the accident, so I take it slow, warming up until it doesn't hurt anymore. I'm motoring, listening to Traffic on Q104.3 singing "Low Spark of High Heeled Boys" on the Walkman, playing air guitar with my free hand. I do a long one, past the luxury yachts in the boat basin and down to the tip of Battery Park City, where I salute the Statue of Liberty and do fifty jumping jacks. *Man on the scene! I feel free!*

I'm smiling at total strangers on the promenade, and they're looking at me funny. Maybe they feel sorry for me. Maybe they know something I refuse to think of in this moment—that all states of bliss are short-lived. That anything that could make a person feel this good probably isn't real. This thought worries me, and soon I'm obsessed. Worst-possible-case scenarios— he's married, has a girlfriend, is an addict, is a compulsive liar, is gay, is unavailable, and will sleep with me before retreating into his mindfuck cave, painfully shrinking my skull to the size of a golf ball.

What's wrong with you? Why so negative? Things are good. Enjoy them. Go with it. You deserve a little happiness.

o o o

Noel requests a meeting. He's been out all night partying with
Yoshi, the Japanese sushi chef from East, around the block.
Yoshi has good energy. He's always smiling even when you
know he's been on a twenty-four-hour drinking binge. He
wears those stilted wooden-Geta sandals with thick white
socks. I've seen him run down the block in those things, looking like a world-class sprinter.

"I've got an intern coming in today," Noel says, a five o'clock
shadow besmirching his usually clean-shaven face. The gel
that ordinarily holds his dark brown hair over the thinning spot
is absent, and his unruly bangs fall over his forehead. "He's
going to trail you and Pablo in the garde-manger. Think you
can teach him the ropes, Slim?"

What's with the Mr. Nice Guy routine? I tell him I'll do my
best.

The intern's name is Jake, and he's taking a year off between
college and grad school to see what the cooking world is all
about. He's from Minnesota and is, unfortunately, not bad-
looking. He flirts with me a little, but this is the way he seems
to get over with just about everyone, including Noel. He scored
this somewhat prestigious internship by smattering his cover
letter to "Chef Noel Barger" with words like "awe," "worship,"
"artistic," and "God." I know this because Noel read the letter
to us a few days before Jake arrived, translating where necessary for Pablo and Javier. To not look like too much of an a-
hole, he made sure to point out that Jake's dubious credentials
included manager at McDonald's and prep cook at the Black

Dog in Martha's Vineyard the summer he graduated from high school.

During my salad-piling demo, I try to be professional, instilling the importance of using just the right amount of salt, pepper, vinaigrette, and assorted herbs. Tossing the leaves with well-washed bare hands, I look over at Jake, who looks bored—is yawning, actually, as if he'd like to move on to bigger and better things.

It's not easy to make a salad stand tall. If it were just mesclun greens, that would be one thing. They're easy to manhandle. You can scrunch and twist them and they'll hold their form. What makes salad piling hell, is Noel's insistence on adding romaine, red leaf, endive, radicchio, and mache to the mix. (The mache is hydroponically grown and for some reason stinks to high heaven. I have brought this to Noel's attention, but he denies the existence of foul odors in much the same way he denies that shrimp have been treated with bleach to make them last longer.) Just try scrunching a crisp leaf of romaine or endive into place—they are the renegades of the sky-high salad, requiring delicate, post-scrunch positioning.

Jake is incapable of attaining salad-presentation perfection. His salad looks more like a molehill than a skyscraper, and he's sighing, behaving as though this whole exercise is a waste of his precious time. He asks, "What's the big deal? Does it really have to look that way?"

I explain, like a good little Tacoma drone, that with Noel, it's all about height. The salad has to look just so. Beets are julienned and fried so they can stick up like spires from mashed potatoes. Rosemary sprigs are used not because they complement a dish but because they look cool, jutting upward like inverted Christmas trees from sautéed filets of mahimahi.

Jake says, "That's stupid. I'm gonna have to give him some shit."

By the end of the week, Jake and Noel have become bosom buddies. Young, handsome, impressionable, and on the smug side, Jake is able to successfully balance ass kissing and giving affectionate shit. Noel fancies Jake as a younger version of himself.

Jake only spends one shift in the garde-manger before Noel has him trailing at the grill and finally the sauté station. On several occasions, he leaves Jake in charge of the kitchen, expediting, in charge of his precious squirt bottles.

This is not the story of the talented young rising star. Jake is still testing the waters, doesn't seem too concerned about cooking as a career. In fact, he tells me he'll apply to business schools in the spring. He and Noel spend much of their time in the kitchen laughing about their four A.M. escapades at Wo Hop in Chinatown.

I decide I can handle Noel flaunting his little buddy in my face. His lack of experience and discernible talent do not seem to be an issue. He is working sauté on O'Shaughnessy's nights off and, because we don't have one, has assumed the sous-chef position. I am eating my heart out. Patience. I must be patient.

o o o

Frank takes me to 1492, a trendy tapas joint in the Lower East Side. He holds out my chair, something my grandfather always used to do at Christmas. This is old-school. This I like.

He orders an expensive bottle of Rioja and we begin our tapas extravaganza with plates of dates wrapped in bacon, langoustines in garlic and butter, chorizo in a tomatoey sauce, and a miniature Spanish tortilla (potato, egg, and onion). Our medium-rare steaks are set before us along with a basket of thinly sliced, golden crisped fries. I'm happy to see that Frank enjoys food—with no mention of any weird hang-ups or allergies.

"I was hoping they'd have sweetbreads on the menu," Frank says.

"You like sweetbreads?" I ask, my heart expanding at the mention of calf thymus.

"I'm an organ man," Frank says, taking a sip of wine.

"I know a place where they make great sautéed sweetbreads," I say.

"You?" he asks, a look of pleased astonishment spreading across his face.

"Love'em," I say. This mutual infatuation with organs bodes well.

Cutting into the steaks with sharp knives, we put morsels in our mouths, close our eyes as if we've died and gone to heaven, chew, and groan, the salty, bloody juices trickling down the backs of our throats.

Frank wants to be famous—appears feverish, in fact, to make his mark. I can relate. The photograph on the front page of the New York Times "Dining Out" section is etched in my mind—a full-body shot of yours truly dressed in chef's whites, my knives laid out before me, looking like a culinary femme fatale. The caption? "Eat Me," an unconventional exposé on a bitchin' girl cook, by Hunter S. Thompson.

Frank's aspirations are no less spectacular. He wants to be the next Bob Marley—a reggae star with, as he puts it, and thank God he's laughing at himself when he says it, "a funky fresh edge."

"I support your dreams, white boy," I say.

"Hey," he says, turning serious, "you've never heard me sing."

"Right," I say, reprimanded. I didn't mean to hurt his feelings. But then Frank says, "I also manage a couple of people."

"Musicians?" I ask.

"Yeah, that's my bread and butter."

"Cool. Anyone I might know?"

"Ever heard of Bang Me?"

"No."

"How about Stunner?"

"Nuh-uh."

"They're two bands that are kind of poised."

"So you're working it," I say. "That's good."

"I'm kind of a workaholic," he shyly asserts.

And, I note, not a dweeby, investment-banking workaholic but an edgy, creative, artistic workaholic. The kind of workaholic we'd all secretly like to be. He's somehow figured out, at the age of twenty-six, how to make a decent living *and* pursue his art. The more he elaborates on the album he's recording with his band, the less glamorous my kitchen career becomes. It is an industry that wants women on their backs, not standing in the trenches with the men, sharing their swollen feet, varicose veins, and oil burns.

By the end of the meal, I'm trying not to think about how much I hate my job. Meeting Frank is a hopeful sign. Sometimes, when nothing's working out the way you hoped, meeting Mr. Right becomes significant.

We hold hands on the table, sip from goblets of thick red wine, and stare dreamily into each other's eyes. Frank asks, "Do you believe in love at first sight?"

"Not usually," I say.

"Me, neither," he says, squeezing my hand, and then, *and then*, he leans over and kisses me on the cheek.

What does it mean? Does it mean that he didn't believe in it and now he does and that's why he's squeezing my hand and kissing me?

My heart's oozing all over the table, but there's more. He graduated from Brown, has a black belt in karate, skis, rock climbs, and has a motorcycle. Is there anything missing? I don't think so.

"My father died in a motorcycle accident," I say, anxious for him to know everything about me.

"Really?" he says. "Are you kidding? I'm so sorry. Wait, are you fucking with me?"

"I don't tell too many people about that," I say.

"I'm so sorry," he says again. "Don't take this the wrong way, but it's not a bad way to go."

"Yeah," I say, "if you've got to."

"And we all do."

Although I offer to help pay, Frank won't even let me see the check. We don't feel the bitter cold on the fifteen-block walk back to my place. I invite Frank up for tea. Sitting next to each other on the couch with large mugs of chamomile, Frank finally leans over, takes the cup from my hand, and places it on the coffee table next to his own. Smoothing his fingers along the back of my neck, he kisses my cheek. My face is flushed. There's a surge of heat between my legs. Frank is delicate, his soft lips nibbling at mine before he allows his tongue to emerge.

Within five minutes, we are smashed together on the couch, panting and sweating in a way that will soon necessitate the removal of clothing—which I'm completely fine with—when

Frank abruptly stops kissing me. Propping himself up on his elbow, he looks at me without speaking for a moment.

"Is something the matter?" I ask.

Shaking his head, looking like he can't believe his great fortune, he says, "No, everything's perfect." He sits up and takes a sip of his tea. "I think I should go," he says, a pained expression stretching across his face.

"Why?" I say, confused. I mean, here I am just lying here, obviously ready to plunge ahead.

"I don't want to leave," he says, standing up and putting on his jacket, "but I'm scared about what might happen if I stay. I'm crazy about you, and I want to take it slow."

I'm sure I've heard something like this before, on more than one occasion, and it makes me feel unwanted and a little insecure, but never mind. He's taking the balanced, mature road, and it's about time I fell for a guy who thinks about more than his penis. I take a sip of tea, stand up, and walk him to the door. "That sounds like a good plan," I say.

Running his fingers through my hair, he massages my scalp with just the right amount of pressure. Leaning down, he kisses me long and deep. I'm too happy to swoon. "I'll call you tomorrow," he says, and waits for me to nod before turning to walk down the five flights.

I sit in the window like Meg Ryan in some Nora Ephron film, praying. *If he looks up at me, it was meant to be.* My heart races as I wait to see his figure on the front steps. There he is, bouncing one, two, three, four—onto the sidewalk. He takes two steps in the wrong direction from where he lives in the East Village, turns, looks up suddenly, and smiling, blows me a kiss.

o o o

Tonight Noel puts me in charge of cooking the mashed potatoes. It is the first time he has let me cook something from
scratch, a garniture for the ginger-glazed pork chops. These
mashed potatoes take on a significance that far outweighs
their station. They are the means by which I will prove I have a
good palate, that I can make the best damned mashed potatoes Noel has ever tasted, that I can in fact *cook*.

I run the peeled boiled Idahos through the potato mill, a
contraption generally found only in professional kitchens. It's
a metal sieve with a handle on top that you turn, forcing the
potatoes down through the tiny holes so that they are made
smooth. I add salt, and butter the way my French culinary teach-
ers taught me, plentifully and without guilt. I perfect the consistency with hot milk, adding more salt and pepper to taste.

When I finish, I smooth the potatoes in the pot with a plastic
spatula and dab little bits of butter on top before sprinkling the
whole thing with more hot milk. This will prevent a skin from
forming on the surface.

Service starts, and Jake struts around the kitchen like his
penis has become too heavy to manage. Sticking a finger in
here, taking a whiff there, he comments on everyone's mise en
place like he's an expert, not some little prick who's decided to
mess around for a couple of months before business school.
Picking up my pot of potatoes, he removes the piece of parch-
ment paper covering the top and, before I can say anything,
swipes his finger through the perfectly smoothed surface. Like
a taster of fine wines, he does the mincing tongue-and-lip

dance, pausing with his eyes toward heaven before proclaim-
ing, "Needs more salt."

Let it here be known that I (along with most cooks and
chefs) am a salt fanatic. Most noncooks are appalled by the
amount of salt they catch me sprinkling into dishes they invari-
ably, upon tasting, agree have great flavor. Seasoning is about
the only thing I feel confident about. The only thing they cannot make me feel I'm not good at. Taking the pot from Jake's
hand, I say, "No," before stirring and smoothing the potatoes
again.

"What do you mean, no?" he asks, looking at me like I'm a
child refusing to wipe my ass.

"I mean no, they don't need more salt."

"Look, I wouldn't have told you they need more salt if I
didn't think they did."

"You're entitled to your opinion, Jake, but I'm in charge of
the potatoes tonight, and I disagree."

Noel is watching, his brow furrowed, his eye cocked. Without saying a word, he marches over to the salt bowl, thrusts his
fat fingers into it, grabs a Jolly Green Giant–sized pinch, lifts
the top off my pot of potatoes and, without tasting them,
throws it in.

This is Noel's way of saying, "You will take orders from an intern because you, Layla Mitchner, and your judgment mean
nothing in my kitchen." It is the ultimate fuck-you.

I am struck dumb. There is no appropriate way for me to respond. I am at once humiliated, ashamed, and angered in such
a primal way that I feel like I've been physically violated, and
there's not a goddamn thing I can do about it. If I were a man,
I might snap, that quick red heat flashing across my face be-

fore I popped Noel a good one on the side of his head. Instead, I stand there speechless, pressure building in my head, mouth hanging open, looking at him in disbelief. Willing my nose not to start bleeding again, I think, *Would now be a good time for me to bend over and grab my ankles?*

o o o

Frank sings "I Believe in Miracles" on the answering machine. He calls twice a day just to see how I'm doing. He invites me over to his place for dinner, and despite his little soliloquy about not wanting to rush things, I am certain we're going to end up in bed together. Julia would say, "Where's the mystique?" But I've never been one to hold things at kissing (and let's face it, neither has she).

Frank lives in a loft with a big metal service elevator. I have brought two hyacinths—one that has blossomed with fragrance, and the other, still closed, waiting to happen. I give these plants symbolic significance.

Hastily taking the plants from my arms, Frank places them on the floor, pulls me in to his chest, and begins kissing me wildly, passionately, as though we haven't kissed in years.

I want him never to stop kissing me this way, and the longer it continues, the more I am reminded of my first sweaty, tongue-wrestling encounter with David Edelstein in the back of a dark theater, not watching *Silver Streak*.

When we pull apart, I notice another person in the room. "Layla, meet Pepe," Frank says, his arm around my shoulder.

Pepe is standing in front of the kitchen counter, a suitcase full of various types of bud open in front of him. "Thai, sense, or regulah?" Pepe asks.

"We were just finishing up a little business," Frank explains.

Pepe looks at the two of us and shakes his head, smiling.

"We haven't seen each other in two days," Frank says.

Pepe seems to understand. "You want to smoke one before I go?" he asks.

Frank looks at me.

"Sure," I say, thankful for something to calm my nerves.

Frank has prepared pasta with meat sauce and a salad. Empty Jars of Ragú are piled in a shopping bag under the kitchen counter. I have brought two bottles of good California Cabernet Sauvignon. It's Sunday, and I don't want us to run out.

Pepe rolls a big cone, and Bob Marley softly sings "Waiting in Vain," while I walk the sweeping loft space. I can't help but ask, "How do you afford this place?"

"The rent's dirt cheap," he calls out from across the room where he stands stirring the sauce.

"How dirt cheap?" I have to know. It's all part of my ongoing quest to discover how other people afford to live in New York City.

"Rent control," he says, putting an end to that discussion. There are several oil paintings of Frank, each exaggerating a certain characteristic—in one his nose is severely crooked, in another his earlobes hang down to his shoulders. The paintings are funny and sad. There is a violin made out of an ax, and what looks like a device for churning butter made out of barbed wire. "Did you make all these?" I ask, impressed.

"Do you like them?" he asks shyly.

"I think they're great," I say. "Especially the self-portraits." I envy his artistic expression, wishing I had more of an outlet myself. When I started cooking, I thought I was getting into a creative field. But professional cooking is more like being on an assembly line. I secretly vow to start taking bass-guitar lessons. I've got to get a sideline.

Pepe, Frank, and I stand around a large wooden chopping block smoking a cigar-sized joint. We're only an eighth of the way through when Pepe picks up his coat and says, "I gotta split," effectively saving me from catatonia.

Steeritup, leetle darlin', steeritup. . . . There's no dining room table, so we sit on the enormous ruby-toned Oriental, bowls of pasta in our laps, a large wooden salad bowl between us. I'm sucking down the wine in an attempt to calm my nerves, but I eat the pasta slowly, savoring the sweet tomatoey sauce. Sometimes, when all you eat is haute cuisine, spaghetti sauce from a jar can taste pretty damn good.

I have just put another bite in my mouth when Frank leans over the salad bowl, waiting patiently, his face directly in front of mine. He lets me chew a little before kissing me on the neck, my soft spot. Goose bumps erupt as he makes his way from my cheek to my lips. Frank has a light touch, delicate and careful, as though he doesn't want to hurt me.

Things heat up quickly. His knee is in the salad bowl and a fork is jabbing painfully into my ass, but neither of us can stop. I am quickly down to my Levi's and bra, something I don't usually wear but bought especially for this occasion.

Picking me up, Frank carries me like they do in the movies to the back of the loft, pushing aside a gauzy scrim on rollers to reveal a king-size bed with Gothic-looking wooden posts jutting out from each corner. This is not the innocent white-sun-dappled bed of my dorm room fantasy. The sheets and duvet are a manly gray, and those posts recall certain scenes in *Dracula* and *Wuthering Heights*.

Placing me on top of it, he pulls off his sweatshirt, revealing his pale, hairless chest. His disheveled hair hangs limply above his shoulders. He looks a little Klaus Kinski-ish—in need of blood, yet sexy, vulnerable, yet ready to please.

Unzipping my jeans, he slowly pulls them off by the bottoms before standing up and taking off his own pants—no underwear. Lying softly on top of me, he gives me wispy kisses all over my face.

This is the moment I've been waiting for, but I am mysteriously incapable of going with it. My brain is on overdrive. I'm thinking petrifying thoughts—what if he doesn't like the way I kiss? Or my body? What if I gross him out? *Someone labotomize me quick.*

When my underwear finally comes off, Frank doesn't mention the Brazilian-bikini-waxed landing strip, which makes me self-conscious. Maybe he thinks it looks stupid? Or perhaps I'm not the first J. Sisters client he's had the privilege of inspecting?

Stop being paranoid. Think of clouds in a blue sky, mountains, sunshine, seascapes. Think pleasant, confirming thoughts. He's clearly into you, you're smitten with him. So you've only known him for one week . . .

Having a man's face in that area can be daunting even at the best of times. *Oh, why can't I just be a free spirit?*

Frank is down there nuzzling, flicking his tongue in what should be the proper area, but try as I might, I can't feel anything. Maybe if he went slower? Faster? Moved a little to the left?

Abruptly withdrawing, Frank turns toward his bedside table.

This is not a good sign.

He pulls out a small box.

"What's that?" I ask.

Quickly and quietly, he begins taking the plastic off the box. "You'll see," he says. "I think you'll like it."

Soon I hear a soft humming, and Frank is holding up a bullet-sized vibrator with a hopeful look in his eye. "I got this for you," he says.

"You did?"

"Yeah, you told me you liked them."

"I did?" I'm pretty sure this isn't true, but I've got to give him points for incentive.

I have become a science experiment—Frank is pushing different buttons with varying degrees of pressure. He wants me to feel good, but my twisted thoughts make me wonder if it's more about his ability to make me feel good than whether or not I actually do.

Frank discourages my attempts at experimentation. He's got to be the one doing things, the one in control. This is something I always imagined I would enjoy. "Frank," I say, putting my hand on his pulsating one, "it's okay. You were doing fine without it."

"I was?" he asks, looking doubtful. The humming stops, and he places his hand on my stomach. "I wasn't so sure."

"Oh, yeah," I say, trying to sound like a girl who's fluent in such things. There's no need for him to know what a sexual retard I've become.

To make up for what I'd like to think is *both* of our discomfort, we become more animated in bed. We are athletes, pinning each other down—grinding and thumping so wildly that five minutes into things, the bed frame breaks, and one corner of the mattress hits the floor. We laugh. Are we not made for each other? Are we not having fun?

Frank comes. I do not. I am so concerned with relaxing that

any sort of real relaxation is impossible. My stomach is in knots. I'm squeezing my ass at least once every two minutes to keep in what I'm hoping and praying isn't foul gas from escaping. My preoccupation sends me rushing into the bathroom under the pretext of brushing my teeth.

"Layla?"

Frank's outside the door. I'm frantically wondering whether I should or should not let him in. The light in the bathroom is bright, the kind in which every cellulite ripple is perfectly outlined. Looking at my pathetic face in the mirror, I think, *I am not fit for human interaction. I should just find myself a nice pack of wolves to hang out with, or a family of bears.*

"Just a second!" I grab a toothbrush. There are three in a cup on the side of the sink. Squirting a neat line of toothpaste on the bristles, I fear I'm taking liberties—what if Frank is one of those guys who can't stand anyone using his toothbrush? *Screw it*, I decide, and begin wildly brushing my teeth. The door is locked.

"Are you okay in there?"

"Yes! Fine! Just brushing my teeth."

"Mind if I come in and take a leak?"

There's no window, no switch for a fan. Brushing my teeth with one hand, I wave the other back and forth behind my butt, do several twirls to try and diffuse things. I could keep him waiting, but I don't want him to think I'm taking a dump or shooting up or anything. I want him to think I'm cool! Squeezing my eyes shut, I spit, pray, swish, and wipe my mouth with a flowery hand towel. Turning the door handle, I open.

Frank is smiling a dreamy smile. When he comes into the scrutinizing light of the bathroom, I notice little red bumps spreading over the outsides of his arms. This imperfection is a flaw I use to put myself at ease. There is a tube of Pantene hair gel sitting on the back of the toilet. I picture Frank coiffing himself in the mirror, arranging his hair just so, worried about how others see him. This offers only temporary relief.

Getting back into bed, I quickly bring the blankets up to my neck. I want everything to be mellow and natural between us. But I've worked myself into such a frenzy that it doesn't feel anywhere near natural, and the rumbling in my lower intestines begins again. My body is rebelling, making noises I would give my life right now to suppress.

Frank gets into bed and puts his arms around me. He's got a peaceful expression on his face. His breath smells like red wine, pot, spaghetti sauce, and salad dressing. What does my breath smell like? Oh yeah, toothpaste. Phew.

Like a sentry over my corpus, I wait vigilantly for the hours to pass, listening to the cars and ambulances and fire trucks on Second Avenue. I make a cast of characters out of the shadows on the walls and ceilings, the way I did when I was a little girl in the top bunk at my grandparents' rose-covered cottage in Nantucket. I used to choreograph plays out of the figures in the chipped paint on the ceiling. There was gaunt grocer Jimmy, old withered Granny Chalkstick, fat farmboy Ernie. The shadows in Frank's loft are not so familiar. They are straighter, perpendicular, less organic, not really people at all, more like machines.

The night is long.

At six I sit up and stretch my arms up like I've never slept better. Like it's totally normal for me to be getting up at this hour. The bed is right across from the kitchen counter, another scrim partitioning it from the windows. Even though it's dark and I can barely see, I don't want to turn on any lights for fear of waking Frank, who is snoring lightly.

Does he keep his coffee in the freezer? Yes! Starbucks French roast. Perfect. Is there a coffee machine? No. How about a coffee filter? Negative. Check cabinets, drawers, under sink. Small strainer lined with a paper towel will work. Boil water, pour coffee in for two, line up mugs, and wait, freezing and naked . . .

Frank wakes with the smell of the coffee. He leans up on his elbow and says, "You're up early. What time is it?"

"Six-fifteen."

He gets up, goes to the bathroom, and comes back out carrying a plaid flannel robe that he places over my shoulders with a squeeze. He kisses the side of my indented hair and gets back into bed. "Mind if I catch a few more winks?"

Mind? Mind? Of course I mind! I have got to get the hell out of here! I'm having an intestinal emergency! I probably shouldn't be making coffee, but I want to go through the motions. I can't just run screaming into the dawn, clenching my ass cheeks. This would be anything but cool.

A sip of coffee might be the end of me bowelwise, but I soldier on. As though nothing could be more normal than making coffee at Frank's place at six-fifteen on a Monday morning.

Frank is lying on his side with the covers pulled up to his ear. After five minutes, he sits up and says, "I can't sleep any more." Flipping the covers off, he gets up and comes toward the kitchen counter. Turning on the light, he exposes my rudimentary coffee-making operation. Putting his arms around my waist from behind and nibbling my ear, he says, "Resourceful."

"Milk? Sugar?" I ask, smiling.

"Just black."

Calm, stay calm. Look cool, like you've been making coffee for Frank all your life. Sauntering over to the huge windows that look out onto Second Avenue, I calmly (Ha!) watch the cars zoom by. There are people walking dogs, homeless men pushing carts, bits of garbage whipping up into small tornadoes. It's gray outside, and even though it's early, I can tell the day will stay that way.

Turning back to survey the loft in the morning light, I notice that aside from our dishes in the middle of the floor and the unmade bed, the place is spotless. I nurse the coffee as long as I can before slurping what I know will be the sip that throws my intestines into convulsions.

"I've got to take off," I say, putting my mug down on the counter and heading toward the closet to fetch my coat. I'm thinking how nice it would be, if I were a normal girl, to languish in bed with my new lover, but it's not to be.

"You're leaving?" he asks, looking hurt.

"I've got to get a head start on the day," I say, unable to think of a good excuse.

"Do I get a kiss?" Frank asks, moving toward me.

I've gotta go, gotta go, gotta go! I smile what I'm hoping isn't the smile of a lunatic but a sexy, early-morning, postcoital smile. Frank kisses me softly, flicking his coffee tongue into my mouth. It feels nice, but I have to cut things short.

He says, "I'll call you later."

"You better," I say, hoping I look like a movie star as I throw on my coat and walk slowly out the door. When I get down onto the street, I'm too focused on the cross-town journey ahead to look up at Frank's window. I wonder later if he was there.

o o o

I do not quit the next day, or the next day or the next, because the gods have decided to smile down on me briefly. By some miracle, Danny O'Shaughnessy and Jake both call in sick for one week running, and because Noel has no one else—and I've been doing most of O'Shaughnessy's mise anyway—Noel grudgingly puts me on sauté. He says, "If I have to save your ass more than once during service, you're back on aps, understand?"

I've been studying every aspect of every dish on sauté for the past two months. How the orzo-filled roasted onions accompany the red snapper in a tart broth dotted with hot chili and cilantro oil. How the pheasant, seared skin-side down and flipped, then finished off in the oven, is served with pumpkin risotto, cranberry coulis, and a side of garlic greens. How the grouper, sautéed in olive oil, then butter, and finished in the oven, lies on a mountain of mashed potatoes surrounded by baby turnips and roasted bits of corn, lightly drizzled with a balsamic reduction.

Ray's portioning out veal chops down in the basement. "Hey, Mommy, want to see what's happening with this veal?"

I stand next to him beaming, too excited to speak, watching him cut between the ribs with his razor-sharp knife, placing each chop on the scale in front of him to be sure he got the ounces right.

"You look like a fat cat today."

"Guess who's working sauté?"

"Ma-ma!" Ray looks almost as excited as I am. "Don't fuck it up, Mommy, show him what you're made of."

"I'm going to."

Because I am determined to do everything by the book, I clean and season the pans by heating them on the fire with a thick layer of kosher salt. Grabbing a folded paper towel with my tongs, I scrub the bottom of the pan with the salt before wiping it with a layer of peanut oil (the rule in professional kitchens, since it doesn't burn as quickly as other oils in high heat).

It's a Wednesday night, and things pick up at around eight o'clock. I am organized and focused, timing the garnitures so that they're perfectly warm when the meat and fish finish cooking. Noel stands watching me, his arms across his chest, eyebrow arched, waiting to find fault.

I'm on fire—clear, organized, and kicking ass. I get the feeling he's disappointed that things are going smoothly. But I'm so grateful he's given me this opportunity that nothing can spoil my high or the goodwill I feel toward him for giving me this chance. I want to impress him. Want to change his mind about me. Show him I'm not just some pussy.

Javier and I work in tandem, like first and second violins in an orchestra, regularly consulting about the timing on our various plates. I like working with Javier (even if he is homophobic, almost coming to blows with Joaquin on several occasions) and fantasize about Noel firing O'Shaughnessy to put me on sauté. The kitchen hasn't run this well in a long time. The rhythm when things are hopping—Javier's steaks are ready with my pheasant and grouper, every item on the plate hot and correctly seasoned—even though there's madness and screaming all around, gives us the sense that for three hours, we have the power to impose order on the world.

For one week straight, I prove to myself, Noel, and the rest of the kitchen that I can work sauté. I feel like an old salt. No biggie. I can do it. But now my fifteen minutes of fame are over. Noel does not fire O'Shaughnessy and put me on sauté. He sends me back to the garde-manger, where it's clear he's willing to let me rot.

I ask for a meeting with Noel. I'm determined not to come off angry or bitter. I want to be gracious, not condemning. Since I've been working with Noel, my desire to cook has dwindled to nothing. I hate him with a passion that can't be healthy.

Joaquin brings me a glass of water, no ice, while I sit in the skylit dining room waiting for Noel to join me. Ho says, "No more bleeding, okay?"

I nod and breathe deeply. I smile at Noel when he sits down, hoping it doesn't look forced. "What can I do for you, Slim?" he asks.

I haven't practiced what I'm going to say, and what comes out astonishes me. "I wanted to let you know that I've really learned a lot working here with you."

He looks surprised. And happy.

I continue, "You've taught me more than you know."

"Well, I'm glad I could do that for you, Slim," he says sincerely.

"I just wanted you to know that before I give notice," I say. For some reason, I am infused with a sense of happiness and calm. I am leaving, and it has always been a belief of mine that you should treat your enemies graciously, in a way that doesn't belie how miserable they've made your life. Until now I have used this tactic primarily on boys who've done me wrong.

Noel looks genuinely relieved. "Leaving so soon?" he says.

It's been over a year, but never mind. "I'm afraid so," I say.

"Well, you've been a great asset to my kitchen."

"Really? Huh. Maybe I'll stay, then," I say, sounding more flippant than I want.

Noel looks nervous and then smiles like a little boy who knows he's been caught in a lie. "Do you have anything else lined up?"

"I've had a few offers," I lie. *The truth is, asshole, you've crushed me so hard, I'm not sure I ever want to work in another kitchen again!*

"Anyplace good?" he asks. I can't be sure if he knows I'm lying, but at this point, I don't really care.

"Yeah." I pause for coyness. I want to fuck with Noel a little, if only to see his reaction. "David Bouley offered me a job on sauté," I say, knowing full well that Noel is unlikely to contact him. Noel worked for Bouley when he was first starting out, and according to rumor, the great master brought him to tears on a regular basis.

Noel shakes his head. He's speechless.

"I've been trailing over there on my nights off."

It's hard to tell if he believes me or not. His face gives away nothing.

"And I just thought you should know that he was really impressed with my skills, which I can only attribute to my time here with you."

Noel jerks his head back, one eyebrow cocked, an "are you shitting me?" look straining across his well-fed face.

Before he can say anything, I continue, "Nice crew over there. I'm really looking forward to it."

Smiling, I politely hold out my hand. Noel takes it and is probably more shocked than I am when he says, "We'll miss you."

o o o

The prospect of love and poverty sets me in motion, and the next morning finds me on the phone energetically dialing up everyone I know in the business. Pinky Fein, a friend of Oscar's, owns the Gilded Lily, a four-star Midtown restaurant renowned for its beggar's purses—paper-thin crepes filled with crème fraîche and Beluga caviar, tied into small bundles with chives, lightly sprayed with edible gold leaf, and presented like candles in a candelabra. Pinky is famous for trolling the restaurant with a pair of handcuffs, fastening diners' hands to the backs of their chairs so they have to eat the purses using only their mouths, while other diners look on, presumably benefiting from the vicarious thrill.

Pinky made his money as an investment banker before getting into the restaurant business. Notwithstanding the tremendous success of the Gilded Lily, Pinky is considered somewhat of a joke because he insists on calling himself the chef, even though he can't boil an egg. And though he's married to Sylvia, the ballbusting business force behind the restaurant, he's kind of a lecher with a penchant for Asian women.

Pinky liked to stop in the kitchen at Tacoma to offer unasked-for advice. One time he sidled up to me with a slick black-and-white advertisement from some industry magazine showing a woman, breasts hidden provocatively by her naked arms, donning a pair of checked chef's leggings. "I think you should consider getting yourself a pair of these," he said with a wink. "In fact, I'll buy them for you myself."

I smiled at him and said, "Thanks, Pinky, that would be great." I'd always felt sorry for him—I'd seen him stumbling around his restaurant red-faced and watery-eyed, drinking a water glass filled to the rim with straight gin. His face would get tighter, his nose thinner, every couple of months.

Sure enough, the next time he showed up at Tacoma, he had a pair of the stretch pants all wrapped up like a present. I was flattered, but I had enough trouble being taken seriously in the kitchen. I could just imagine what the guys would say if I pranced around in what amounted to a pair of checked tights.

Noel got a huge kick out of it, thought the tights were an excellent idea—"Come on, Slim, show us what you've got." The bastard. They remain in the bottom of my closet to this day.

Pinky tells me he doesn't have anything at the Gilded Lily, but he'll make a few calls to some of his friends over at Eateries Incorporated, the company that owns contracts for many of the city's museums, theaters, and opera houses. "You don't mind working freelance, right?"

"Right," I say.

"Good."

The chef at Lincoln Center calls that afternoon to ask if I can work a sit-down dinner for 250 people next week—$20 an hour. "I'll be there," I say.

o o o

It's getting to be that time again, and $1,000 to share a tiny dwelling in the West Village is starting to feel like a major rip-off, especially now that I've prematurely cut myself off from my steady source of income. I was living hand-to-mouth as it was with a full-time job, health benefits, and a 401(k). Now that I'm freelancing, I've got only as much money as my next gig, and it feels like I'll never make another penny as long as I live.

I foolishly decide to call up Julia and ask for a loan. She agrees to lend me $500. I will be paying her back with interest. Literally. She wants to know if I plan on ever working again, or is she supposed to support me for the rest of my life? What was I thinking when I embarked on this whole cooking fiasco, anyway? Didn't I know it wasn't a moneymaking proposition?

What about acting? I want to ask. I guess she's the only one allowed to dream and take chances. And what chances has she ever really taken? She's never had to work a day in her life!

Julia is angry. Disappointed. She tells me I better marry a sugar daddy if I am to continue in this way. I think what a lot of good that did her and almost make the mistake of telling her so. She begins ticking off items on the "Why Layla Is a Bad Person" list. About how humiliated she was when I got busted in boarding school for having a gallon bottle of Popov in a duffel under my bed. About the married man who stole my youth. About *wasting* three years of my life *bumming around* out west. About how she's *always* having to bail me out when the going gets tough. About all of the no-good losers I ever dated who weren't fit to tie my shoes.

But that's not all. I am lazy, have always gotten by with minimal effort, and therefore know very little about the *important things in life.* I am selfish and slovenly. I do not make the best of my upbringing. I use people but at the same time am too generous and trusting, so bad people wind up taking advantage of me. I, according to my mother, am a loser with a capital "L."

After a lifetime of listening to this sort of thing, I've come to believe she may have a point. I let her ramble on about what a horrible human being I am until she comes to her grand finale, the climactic conclusion. Which is?

"I loved you too much."

But enough about that. She's going to Aspen with Paolo for some spring skiing. She'd love to invite me but is sure I'll be too busy looking for a job.

All this for $500. I should have gone to the meatpacking and pulled a couple of tricks. It would have been easier to swallow.

o o o

"Hey, guess who won the green-card lottery?" Gustav looks happier than I've ever seen him. We are sitting at the bar at Blue Ribbon. Gustav has ordered a bottle of Taittinger and a large plate of oysters.

"You *won* it?"

"Not just me, a bunch of people."

"How many do they give out?"

"I don't know, exactly. A few-eh. You know what this means?"

"No."

"It means I never have to go home and see that stinking bastard again. Cheers!" Clinking my glass, he tips his head back and takes two large gulps.

"What stinking bastard?" I ask, holding the glass by the stem and sipping delicately.

"Ah, forgedit. He's not worth my breath." Gulp. Refill. Flicking his finger at the top of his glass a couple of times, Gustav looks at me and says, "He was a mean son of a bitch-eh. Used to kick the shit out of me. My mother, too. I left home when I was sixteen. Did I ever tell you?"

I shake my head. "I think I would have remembered." This is the first time Gustav has ever spoken of his family back in Austria.

"I worked at my uncle's gas station. You know, there they have restaurants and gas stations combined. That's where I learned to cook."

"Your dad hit you?"

"Hit," he says, looking at me, his expression turning to anger. "More like—how do you say?"

" 'Pummel'?"

"What's 'poomel'?"

"To beat vigorously."

"Yeah, that's more like it-eh. He broke this finger on my face," he says, bending his middle finger just short of flipping me off and placing it against his jaw. "He's old now, though. He'll die soon, I hope."

It's the first time anyone's ever told me he wishes a parent dead, and I breathe out, relieved. Gustav's admission allows me to believe momentarily that I'm not as evil as I thought.

"I've been wanting him to die ever since I was born-eh."

"Maybe you'll feel differently when he really does die," I say, feeling a slight heart palpitation as I think of my own dead father, who, I have to admit, is still sort of on my shit list.

"Oh no," he says, shaking his head and taking a couple more sips of champagne. "No way! I will be the happiest man alive, I can assure you of that!"

There is a large Polynesian behind the bar with a neoprene bandage over his elbow and forearm. He's not kidding around when he tells us he's got shucker's elbow. He's opening up oysters like nobody's business, dislocating the muscles from their shells, arranging them on an ice platter and squeezing it in between glasses and bottles on the bar in front of us. I white trashily spoon a dab of cocktail sauce on mine, clink shells with

Gustav. We loudly slurp the oysters and their ice-cold salty juice down the backs of our throats.

"That's good-eh. You know how they make pearls?"

"They start as a grain of sand, right?"

"A grain of sand, anything that's not supposed to be in there, an irritation, they build up the pearl to cover the irritation. That's what I want to do with my life. Make something good out of something bad-eh . . . Hey," he says, as though he's just thought of it, "I saw a For Rent sign at this diner along the West Side Highway. I want to show it to you."

"You want to start a place?"

"Yeah. Gustav's."

"You mean Layla's?"

"How about just . . . Gustav's?"

"Layla's is catchier. Look, Gustav, are you going to give me the scoop on this place or what? Are you serious?"

"As a heart attack-eh."

"I thought you didn't want to be a chef."

"I don't want to be the chef of someone else's restaurant. My own place, that's a different story."

"And how do you plan to fund this whole thing?"

"We'll need to get some backers. I might be able to get my uncle interested. Maybe Oscar would help. What about you? You think your mother would be interested?"

"I doubt it."

"She's got money though, right?"

"Yeah. But she doesn't like to share."

"What's her name again?"

"Julia."

"What if we called it Julia's?"

"She might go for it."

By the end of the night, Gustav and I have a plan to see the place the next day. As always, he takes care of the bill.

Gustav walks me to my bike and kisses me good night on the cheek. Almost as an afterthought, he says, "I'm going to meet Gem."

It's past eleven o'clock. "Gem?"

"You know, the beauty from the Thai place? The hostess?"

"You guys are going out?"

"Didn't I tell you-eh?"

"Must have slipped your mind. I can't believe she'd go out with a dog like you."

Gustav clutches his heart in mock insult. "Dog? Me?"

Part of me is kidding and part isn't. I don't like the idea of my guy friends having girlfriends. I want to secretly believe they're all just holding their breath until the day I deign to sleep with them. "Have fun," I say.

"Oh, I will-eh," he says, winking. "She's a dancer. Did I tell you? Very flexible."

"That's nice," I say, recalling Gem—small, athletic, long, silky black hair—quite beautiful. The thought of Gustav and Gem in bed together suddenly makes me very sad. Not because I want to be in bed with Gustav, but because it's difficult for me to accept other people's happiness in love when I'm feeling something like dread.

I try not to think about whether Frank has called but can't help it. Part of the reason I went out with Gustav in the first place was to get myself out of the apartment, away from the phone, anxiously awaiting Frank's call. It's been two days, and I still haven't gotten the requisite postsex check-in.

o o o

There is a man, a really attractive, rich-looking guy, sitting on the futon next to Jamie when I get home. He's got on a perfectly pressed white cotton oxford and a pair of slacks. Jamie is decked in a tight-fitting little black dress, her matching yellow and black Gucci alligator pumps lying suggestively by the coffee table. Is it possible to feel underdressed in your own home?

There are partially filled champagne flutes and a large silver ice bucket with a frosty bottle of Cristal on the coffee table. Van Morrison softly sings "And It Stoned Me" in the background. Jamie smiles as though she's really happy to see me. "Hey, Layla, I want you to meet Tom."

"Hi, Tom."

"Layla, nice to meet you," Tom says. "Can I offer you a glass of champagne?" He stands and graciously stretches out his arm, indicating I should join their lovefest on the couch.

"Sure," I say, thinking, *Lovers and champagne are not exactly what I need right now.* "Has anyone called for me?" I ask. I don't want either of them to know how obsessed I am about getting that call.

Jamie shakes her head with a pitying smile. "Sorry, sweetie, no. Here, sit down with us, tell us what's going on."

Ever since my nosebleed, Jamie and I have been getting along. This might have something to do with the fact that we haven't seen all that much of each other, which I now realize might have something to do with Tom. "Nothing's going on."

"Well, I did happen to notice that someone didn't spend the night here on Sunday."

"Did you?" I ask, hoping she'll drop it.

"Yes, I did."

"New guy?" Tom asks.

"I guess you could say that," I say.

"He's totally into her," Jamie explains. "Sang 'I Believe in Miracles' on the answering machine and everything." She's looking at Tom like *This guy really meant it.*

"Impressive," Tom says in a way that makes me wonder whether he's joking. "Has he called?"

"No," I say.

"He'll call," Jamie says. "He's crazy about you, and well he should be!"

What is it with her tonight? I'm completely devastated that Frank hasn't called. I can feel myself losing that tentative grip on reality, slipping into psychotic basket-casedom. Instead of shutting myself up in my bedroom and crying the night away, as I feel like doing, I begin to ramble—describing every nuance, situation, and sentence that has occurred between Frank and me. They graciously laugh. Obsessive people can be entertaining in small doses.

"Give it some time," Tom says, like he's known me for years.

"I know," I say, "it's hard."

"You've got to play it cool," Jamie says.

"Good advice," Tom says.

"Is that what you two are doing?" I ask, wondering just what the hell their story is.

"You bet," Tom answers, putting his arm around Jamie.

Why do I want to get tanked all of a sudden? Better have a cigarette. Suddenly I see that despite her prissy, wafer-thin demeanor, Jamie is far more cool and comfortable with this incredibly nice and stable-seeming Tom than I could ever be with

Frank. I am a nervous, jittery failure. Jamie tosses her pumps and drinks champagne. I run to the bathroom frantically holding back farts.

Tom says, "An attractive girl like you, he'd be crazy to let you go."

I give Tom an "Oh, please" look, because attractive is the last thing I feel. "His letting me go isn't part of my plan," I say. "If anyone's letting anyone go, it'll be *me* letting go of him."

Tom shrugs.

"Why are you shrugging?" I ask, panicked.

"Don't you think you might be rushing things a little?"

"Tom, honey, you've got to understand the female psyche," Jamie says.

"Please," he says, "fill me in."

"Well, women tend to put more of themselves into a relationship, become more invested. Right, Lay?"

"Right."

The phone rings. "The phone's ringing!" I shriek.

"Calm down," Tom says, laughing at me.

"Let it ring three times," Jamie says, sharing in my excitement.

I pick up after the third ring. There is a click, and the line goes dead. Holding the phone up, I say, "Must have been a wrong number."

"Oh, sweetie, I'm sorry."

"Have another glass of champagne," Tom says helpfully.

"Do you have any friends?" I ask.

"I've got a bunch," Tom says, pouring me another glass.

"Good. By the way, what are we celebrating?"

The two of them shine at each other, flushed and blissful, before Jamie turns to me and breathlessly blurts, "Our engagement!" Bending into Tom, she kisses him on the lips before hoisting up her skinny, well-manicured hand and wiggling a blindingly huge emerald-cut diamond in my direction.

"You're engaged? When did you start going out!" I scream, causing Jamie and Tom to jump slightly. "Sorry," I quickly manage, "it's just so exciting." *I am now going to walk into the Hudson River without delay.*

"We've been together for what, about three months now?" Tom says.

"Three months," I say, trancelike.

"When you know, you know," Jamie sings.

"I guess so," I say, hoping I don't sound like sour grapes.

When the bottle of champagne is finished, I try to get Tom and Jamie to join me in some Courvoisier, but they decline. After waving good night, they close Jamie's bedroom door, leaving me alone and desperate on the couch, clutching the neck of the bottle. Why bother with a glass? I uncork, tilt, and take a large, burning gulp. "Let it burn," Grampie Mitchner used to say, and I do. I let it burn again and again until I'm tired and sad and feel like dying. I go to the bathroom and brush my teeth. One must always keep up appearances.

By the time I crawl into bed, I'm feeling so sorry for myself that I've begun to cry quietly, eyes squinched, mouth curling up at the sides in an anguished smile. I can hear soft voices through the wall. They are talking, laughing quietly.

Why haven't you called, Frank? Why?

The party of desperation has barely begun when the phone rings again. Cutting the whimpering short, I get up and crack open the door. The machine picks up after four rings. The clock on the wall says twelve-thirty.

"Hey, Layla, it's Frank." He sounds tired. "Sorry it's so late. I just got done recording. We rented the space by the hour, and I couldn't make any calls until now. I thought I might catch you, but I guess you're out. I'll try you again tomorrow."

Out? Out doing what? Partying at Lotus with my fabulous friends? If only. The wave of relief that crashes over me is warm and tropical. He's not blowing me off! He was recording! Of course he was. Probably hasn't had a single moment to himself. Just hearing his voice calms me, lets me know everything's going to be okay. I go over to the answering machine and replay the message five times, listening for hints in Frank's voice. Is he lying? Could he really not find a minute to call during two whole days? Doesn't "I'll call you later" usually mean, like, later that day?

I decide to take him at his word. The alternative would be too tragic. I disco down with the dining nook table, feeling hopeful for the first time since I last saw him. Getting back into bed, I try to sleep, but the cognac has made it difficult. I have to keep getting up to drink water from the bathroom faucet and pee. I finally fall into a disturbed sleep filled with dreams in which I'm running away from someone who wishes to harm me. I shoot, but the bullets peter out and do a nosedive just before hitting their target. When I dial for help, I keep messing up the number on the rotary phone. I can't get through.

o o o

Guzzling coffee, I pace the apartment and agonize over whether or not to call Frank back. It's not nice not to call someone back when he's left a message . . . but it's only eight-thirty, and I don't want him thinking I'm too eager. . . . I'll have to wait at least a half hour. After such a late night, he should be at home.

At nine, I call. The phone rings past four and his voice comes on, "Do what you need to do at the beep."

For a split second, I consider hanging up. Why isn't he there? Is he screening? "Hello Frank, it's Layla Mitchner call-ing." *Just in case he forgot which Layla?* "Got your message last night, thanks for calling." *Nice trembling falsetto.* "I'll be out most of the day, but give me a call when you get a chance. Hopefully we'll get to talk soon."

Silky smooth. My voice was spanning octaves like Mariah Carey singing the national anthem. What is it about this guy that turns me into Jell-O? I just hope and pray he doesn't catch on.

Gustav shouts from the street, and I buzz him up. I can hear him clumping up all five flights with his Rollerblades on. His blond mullet moves up and around the landing until he's fac-ing me, red and sweaty. "You look good-eh," he says, walking like Frankenstein toward me and kissing me on the cheek.

"Not this morning, Gustav, I'm not in the mood."

"What? I'm serious!"

"I'm touched," I say.

"You should be," he says. He plops down on the futon in the living area and catches his breath. "By the way-eh, I forgot to tell you last night. That creep, O'Fuckhead?"

"O'Dickwad? What did he do now?"

"You're going to love this story. Apparently, Noel comes in one afternoon to experiment with this new recipe for focaccia, and the Hobart's missing."

"Nooo," I say, getting excited. "That thing's *huge*."

"Naturally, after the knife incident, Noel goes to O'Shaugh-nessy, who of course denies having anything to do with it. So

Noel's trying to figure out what he's going to do—does he go to the guy's apartment looking for the mixer or what-eh? In the meantime, the guy's still doing the blow during service, and one of his posse—remember that night when we were getting high?"

"How could I forget?"

"One of those Tommy guys shows up at the window on a Friday night, I'm working sauté and the kitchen's in the serious weeds—"

"Gustav, Jesus—is it good or bad?"

"Very bad," he says, beaming. "The Tommy guy pulls a fucking gun on Noel through the pickup window, tells him to get O'Shitface out where he can see him. The customers at the restaurant don't know what's going on at first, but some uptight business lady sees the gun flashing and starts to scream. Oscar's at the bar, so fucked up he's hardly seeing straight, and Noel, the pussy-eh, is practically shitting his pants. Before Noel can say anything, Javier grabs Danny by the back of his jacket and tries throwing him out of the kitchen. O'Dirtbag doesn't want to meet his death so quickly, ah? He's putting up a fight, swinging madly at Javier"—Gustav swings his fists in front of him to demonstrate—"and Tommy Boy blasts the sprinkler system—you know the chemical shower for when there's a fire? That white foamy smelly shit is spraying all over the kitchen. Customers are fleeing for their lives! It was beautiful-eh."

"Yeah, and then what?"

"What do you mean 'and then what'? You need more?"

"Did Danny get shot or what?"

"I don't even want to know what happened to Danny. The

Tommy guy hauled him out of the restaurant, waving his pistol around like a cowboy, threw him into the back of a black Lexus, and sped away."

"Shit."

"*Yeah*, shit."

Gustav asks me if I want to go skiing with him up at Hunter this weekend, and rather than tell him I have no money, I say, "I hate Hunter. I refuse to ski there." Which is also true.

"Hey," he says, "I grew up in the Austrian Alps, and you don't see me looking down my nose-eh."

"The West is the best," I say.

"So what are you doing here, then?"

"I met a guy."

"Nah!" he says in disbelief. "You?"

"Why is that so hard for you to believe?" I ask.

"I don't know-eh," he says, shaking his head. "It's not." Looking at my face and seeing I'm hurt, he musses up my hair and says, "Ah, come on! I didn't mean anything. . . . So who's the guy?"

"Someone I met at the Hogs."

"De Hogs!" he says. "You better let me check him out, then." Gustav puts his hand on my shoulder and moves it softly back and forth. I'm expecting something sweet, something sincere. "You fucking him?"

"That's none of your fucking business!"

"You're not fucking him."

"I might be."

"No, you're not," Gustav says with finality. "Believe me, I'd know."

"I'm sure you would," I say.

"Babe? When are you going to let Gustav make you a happy woman?"

"Um, let me see," I say, index finger on the side of my chin, lips pressed to the opposite side of my face, "never?"

"You don't know what you're missing-eh."

"Oh, I'm pretty sure I do, and besides, you know I'd just break your heart."

Gustav clutches his chest in mock pain. Standing up, he wobbles and says, "Vamanos."

I am hungover from the cognac. Outside, the fresh air feels good—biting, the wind blowing off the Hudson. The sun is out, almost making it a nice day. Gustav puts his arm around me when I start to shiver. "After this, I'll take you to lunch, okay?"

"Okay," I say. Gustav never lets me pay for anything. Says it's the Austrian way. I'm not so sure, but I let him. I want to make Julia's money last.

"Aren't you going to ask me how my night was?" he asks.

"I'm sure it was lovely," I say. I really don't want to hear the details.

"First we did some yoga moves together. She's a part-time instructor so-eh—"

"That would explain the flexibility."

"Fuggedaboutit," Gustav says, trying to sound like Joe Pesci but sounding even more like Arnold.

In the distance, my dream diner comes into view—chrome, with a big non-working neon arrow on the roof pointing down to a sign that says, "Eat Here." Gustav hands me his cell phone, points to the number on the For Rent sign, and says, "You call."

I take it from him and dial.

"Big Apple Diner?" a woman's voice answers.

"Hello, my name is Layla Mitchner, and I'm calling about the diner for rent on the West Side Highway?"

"Just a second." I hear a muffled voice in the background calling, "Eddie! Someone about the diner!"

A man gets on. "Hello?"

"Hi, this is Layla Mitchner, I'm interested in speaking to you about the diner for rent?"

"Oh sure. *Terrific.* You want to see it?"

"Me and my partner are standing in front of it right now."

"Oh, okay, great. I'm up at my other place, the Big Apple. I can be down there in fifteen minutes. How does that sound?"

"Great. See you then." After hanging up, I look at Gustav and, jumping up and down to fend off the cold, say, "He's coming."

"Now?"

"Yeah."

"Let's see if we can see anything through the windows."

There are several dirty glasses and cups strewn on the bar and a few of the tables. A bucket with a mop sits idly in the aisle. Gustav wants to climb a pole up to the roof so he can check out the structure, but I convince him not to. He's calculating, thinking out loud. "What's the bucket there for? Could be a leak in the ceiling. . . . "

Eddie shows up. He looks like a man who wants to sell us a bridge. He wears a reddish piece that doesn't quite match the gray on the sides. He starts talking immediately. "So, you two are interested in turning this into a restaurant? That's great, just great. It would be the perfect place. I had my son in here before. He owned a catering company called Film Food—did a crazy, crazy business. But you know how kids can be. He decided he wanted to be the one *making* the films, not feeding the crew and actors, know what I mean? Couldn't say I blamed him. He's been out in Hollywood now a couple of months. Just heard from him yesterday, in fact, he tells me he might've sold a script."

Gustav's checking out the grill, the oven, the dishwasher, getting his whole upper body inside to inspect, while I look around at the decor, thinking about what the place could look like if we fixed it up a little. I envision a trendy upscale diner, not too expensive, where you can get well-made, beautifully pre-sented homestyle cooking—savory meat loaf, steaks, roasted chicken, mashed potatoes and gravy, wiener schnitzel, pie à la mode, little baskets of five different kinds of homemade bread. Gustav and I will do the cooking while a legion of babes remi-niscent of the girls in Robert Palmer's "Simply Irresistible" video wait tables and give the place that funky, hip aura. Our place will be the next hot thing.

Gustav barely speaks to the guy. Neither of us can get a word in edgewise.

"So I've got this fifty-year lease on the place, and what I could do for you is have my lawyer draw up a sublease contract—three thousand a month. We can do a monthly, yearly, what-ever you want. It's a great deal."

Gustav finally cuts him off, saying, "Thanks, we'll give you a call."

Walking the narrow cobblestoned streets, we make our way to Home, a restaurant on Cornelia Street. Gustav is unusually quiet. As soon as we slide into a booth, he says, "I don't trust that guy-eh. The place has been sitting empty a long time, that much anyone could see. He was too eager. If it's such a great place for a restaurant, how come there isn't one there yet?"

"That's where we come in."

"I don't think so, babe. When something stinks, this big

honker smells it," he says, pointing to his large, off-center nose. "The roof was cracked all over the place, the stove needed to be replaced. It would take a lot of money. That's why the rent is so cheap."

"It was really that bad?" I ask.

"It wasn't good, that much a blind man could see. We'll keep looking, though-ah? What are you having?"

"A bacon cheeseburger."

"Me, too."

The message light is blinking when I get home. *Please God, let it be Frank. Don't let me down. Do not let me down, God.* "Hey, Layla, Frank here."

Yes!

"It looks like it's gonna be another late night. How about dinner on Friday?"

It's Monday. If I weren't so fucking stupid, I'd be absolutely positive Frank was blowing me off. Well, two can play that game. I decide not to return his call. If he wants to see me, he can damn well make an effort. Otherwise, I've got a life to lead. People to see. I've got lots of friends to hang out with, plenty of business to attend to. I'm determined to fight fire with fire. Already I'm at war, and I'm not even sure why. The thing is, if Frank isn't blowing me off, then I'm being a bitch. If he is blowing me off, then I don't ever want to see him again. One thing's for sure, I am growing more desperate by the day.

o o o

I report to the basement at Lincoln Center, where the cooks are working in a hallway because the kitchen is too small to accommodate both regular service and special parties. Cutting boards are set up on rolling carts pushed against the wall, where raw scraps of salmon are being minced into tartar by a platoon of Mexicans.

The chef puts me on spinach duty with Maxine, who's skinny and awkward-looking with limp, mousy brown hair. She's around my age but looks sixteen and has been cooking professionally since she was about that old. Her dream is to be the chef on a private yacht in the Mediterranean, but until then she freelances parties like this one.

The two of us stand in the hallway destemming spinach and loading it into plastic bags. Leaf by leaf, Maxine recounts her life story. "I was living in London with my husband and two kids . . ."

She looks so young, I can't believe she's married, much less has kids. It is a sordid tale of love, drink, and deceit, the details of which become muddier and muddier by the minute. It's not the kind of thing I want to prompt her on, though—"Wait, you started an affair with the cleaning lady, she left you for your husband, they married and took your kids away?"—so I keep my mouth shut and listen.

By four o'clock, the kitchen clears out, and we take the bags of spinach to the sink for washing, after which we steam it in large pans, reducing the volume dramatically. Robert, the chef, is a nice guy, but even though he lacks a Noel-sized ego, he still has preconceived notions about what girls should do in kitchens. While the guys are searing filet mignons, grilling chicken breasts, poaching salmons, putting the final touches to the Bordelaise, soy ginger, and creamy dill sauces, Maxine and I stand in the hallway squeezing water out of trayfuls of steamed spinach.

But Robert's one of those chefs who doesn't consider anything beneath him, which makes me feel a little bit better about being put on spinach duty. He's a big bear of a guy, with a full beard and rubber Birkenstock clogs. Moving from cook to cook, he helps with every phase of preparation and finally ends up in the hallway with Maxine and me. "Where have you worked?" he asks me.

"Most recently Tacoma," I say.

"Ooh. Noel Barger," he says, commiserating.

"Yeah," I say.

"Enough said," he says, holding up a spinach-flecked hand.

"What's the deal with Noel Barger?" Maxine asks.

"Let's just say he got a little too big for his britches," Robert says, piquing my interest.

"What do you mean?" I ask, waiting smugly for someone else in the business to confirm what I already know.

"You heard what happened at Tacoma, right?"

"Oh, yeah," I say. "He's lucky he didn't get a cap in his ass."

"I think we're thinking of two different stories," Robert says, chuckling.

"What are you talking about?" I ask, confused.

"I heard," Robert says, scooping up a large fistful of spinach and squeezing green water out of it with both hands, "that Oscar found a new boyfriend."

"WHAT?"

"You didn't know?" Robert asks, laughing.

My jaw has dropped, and I'm standing there bug-eyed. "Noel is *not* gay," I say, more out of disbelief than in defense of his masculinity.

"Says you," Robert says. "Let's just say that Oscar drives a hard bargain, shall we?"

"Oh, please."

"Hey, I've heard of guys doing worse things to get chef's positions."

Feeling sorry for Noel is about the last thing I expected, but when Robert tells me Oscar canned him and he can't get a job anywhere, that's exactly how I feel. That is, until Robert hauls over a tray of garlic heads and tells us to degerm every clove— i.e., remove the green indigestible section in the middle. Then I just feel sorry for me and Maxine.

o o o

Abdul, the daytime sauté guy at Tacoma, offers to hook me up with Wayne Nish at March. Jimmy, the guy who makes Tacoma's bread, used to work with Jean Georges. Ray says his buddy Mikey, the fish guy, would be a good person for me to see because he supposedly knows everybody. Gustav thinks I should meet a girl chef named Laurie who runs a place called West 12th.

Wayne Nish is handsome, polite, and spends the afternoon showing me around March's kitchen. The sauté cook is a Caribbean guy named Nathaniel who used to work for Pinky at the Gilded Lily. Nathaniel is somewhat of a legend, known not only for being able to drink life-threatening quantities of rum while pumping out exquisite meals, but for the prodigious size of his penis.

I like Wayne. Contrary to the popular notion of a chef needing to be wound up and hotheaded, he has an extremely soothing presence. Unfortunately, he doesn't have any open positions. He'll call me if anything turns up.

Jean Georges is impossible to get ahold of.

I meet Mikey, the fish guy, at the University Club, where I am allowed in for only one drink because I'm a girl and I'm not wearing a skirt. Mikey takes me along his rounds of the various restaurants so that I can meet chefs, while he drops off long white envelopes stuffed with cash. In an attempt not to look like a hillbilly, I've got on my one good pair of Joseph pants, a fitted Brooks Brothers shirt, the mocha boots, and a long coat.

One chef, a French guy with longish, greasy hair, creased, hard-drinking skin, and a Gauloise hanging out of the corner of his mouth, looks haggard as he accepts his envelope—like this is just one more indignity he's got to endure in a bitter life full of disappointment. Mikey introduces me and tells him I'm a graduate of the Cordon Bleu. His eyes widen, amused. "Le Cordon Bleu, ah? *C'est quoi ça?*"

"What's he sayin'?" Mikey asks.

"He wants to know what that is," I say.

"Come on, man," Mikey says, punching the chef's shoulder, "you know, the cooking school—Lay Cord-*on* Blue! I'm sayin' it right, right?" he asks, looking at me.

I nod.

"Ah bon? C'est une école?"

Most French people I've met have no idea that Le Cordon Bleu is a cooking school. To them, it is nothing more than a description signifying that something is the best. *"Oui, c'est ça,"* I say, suddenly seeing myself through this man's eyes. I am a spoiled little American girl who's decided to slum it in kitchens for a while, nothing more. I cannot buy what he has given his whole miserable life to acquire.

Mikey and I have fun together, drinking Amstel Lights in empty bars. At Baci, a large older man comes over and gives

Mikey a kiss on both cheeks. When he's no longer in earshot, Mikey whispers, "That's Uncle Dom. Just got out of prison. See that Rolex? He got it off the guy while he was dying."

After the evening with Mikey, I feel no closer to having a job, but at least I'm having fun. He's driving me home in a white Ford Explorer, and on an impulse, I ask him to take me to Frank's place. As we approach, I strain to see whether the lights are on, but the windows are dark.

"Shake?" Mikey says, holding his hand out.

I grab it firmly, like a businessman doing a deal.

"I'll make some calls, see what I can do."

"Thanks, Mikey, that would be great. I gave you my number, right?"

"Got it."

I walk up to the buzzer and stand there staring at it. Mikey's still waiting to make sure I get inside okay, so I turn, wave at him, and smile like I'm all set. I do not want to ring the buzzer—it smacks of weakness and desperation. But my hand bolts up as though unattached to my body and hovers over the small metal square. *Don't do it!*

Looking down the block, I see an awning and head toward it. I have no idea what I'm doing or even thinking. I have to see Frank, or at least talk to him. All of this answering-machine business is starting to make me foam at the mouth. We haven't had a real conversation since we slept together. I feel like he's blowing me off without ever having given me a chance. That somehow, he hasn't gotten to see the real me, and if we could just spend some time together, I would be able to relax and not be all crazy and gassy and weird. I would be cool and confident and lovable.

The doorman opens the door, and I walk in.

After watching me wring my hands for several minutes in the lobby while I debate the pros and cons of the buzzer press, the doorman, who seems to have taken a grandfatherly interest in me, suggests I write him a note.

"Here, write 'im this," he says, rifling through his podium drawer for a pen and piece of paper. " 'Roses are red, violets are blue, I'm at East Ninth Street, and I wish you were, too.' "

I stand frozen, pen poised over paper. *Dear Frank. Frank—. Hi Frank. Hey, Big Guy. To Master Frank Stillman . . .* Ah, fuck it.

Thanking the doorman, I head out into the windy night, wishing I wasn't such a coward. Crossing Second Avenue, I force myself to look back up at the window. It's still dark. Checking my watch, I see it's after one. Maybe he's asleep?

There's a message from Frank on the machine when I get home. "Hey, Lay. I just wanted to call and tell you I've been thinking about you. Sorry I've been working so much, I miss you. . . . We'll have fun together this weekend, okay? Sleep tight, don't let the bedbugs bite. . . ."

I need to relax.

o o o

Jamie informs me that she will be moving in with Tom at the end of May. "Not to worry though, sweetie, I'm going to help you find someone to take my place."

I don't want anyone to take her place. I've gotten used to Jamie. I don't want to think about it. Come to think of it, I don't want to think about anything—my job, Frank, Julia. It's times like these that can really push a person over the edge. I imag-

ine people must commit suicide over things that may not necessarily be worth dying over. Maybe it just strikes some people as being easier to off themselves than it is to find another
roommate, boyfriend, mother.

The phone rings. Fighting my preoccupation with what
Frank thinks of me, I pick it up after the first ring—fucked if I
care.

"Puppy! You're home! I left you a message yesterday, did
you get it?"

Julia. "Um, no, I didn't. Jamie must have forgotten to tell
me." *Or maybe I'm just sick of being your voodoo doll?*

"Well, the Bernsteins have invited Paolo and me to their
Seder this year, and I thought it might be nice if you came, too."

I picture the strapping Paolo, his long dark hair pulled back
into a ponytail, a velvet yarmulke on his head. Passover is the
only Jewish holiday Julia celebrates. My childhood memories of
it consist mainly of long, drawn-out prayer, growling stom-
achs, parsley, salt water, and smelly gefilte fish. "I can't," I say.

Pregnant pause. "I'm sorry to hear that," she says, sounding
mortally wounded.

Every once in a while, Julia likes to try and pretend we're a
family. I have been good about preserving this myth in the
past, but I'm over it. Little things have been occurring to me,
like, why am I such a nutjob? Do I really want to be a cook? How
is it that I've put all of my eggs in some basket I picked up at
Hogs & Heifers two weeks ago? Why am I this way? And whose
fault is it? I blame Julia.

"So how's everything?" I ask, trying to change the subject.

"Oh, everything's just splendiferous. I've been doing some
work in my apartment, and this beautiful Persian rug I bought
a month ago—it was incredibly expensive, but it just doesn't

go with the color scheme in the living room. I'm wondering, would you like to borrow it?"

"You need a place to store it."

"It might fit nicely into your living room. I'm not sure what your colors are—"

"I don't have any colors."

"Don't be ridiculous, puppy, every room has a color scheme."

"Well, you've never been to my apartment, but I can assure you, there is no color scheme," I say, thinking of the worn gray hooked rug that Jamie's grandmother gave her, our sole nod to interior decoration.

"Maybe you'd like to come and see what I've done to my place? You won't believe the transformation. I put in new windows, redid the kitchen. The Polish tile man told me I had a real knack for design. Told me that if I ever wanted to get into business with him—"

"Sounds like you've got a gift."

"By the way, how's the job search going?"

"Really well," I say. "I've been getting offers all over town."

"When you were little, you wanted to be a doctor."

"I don't remember that," I say, blood pulsating in my temples.

"Well, maybe you'll marry one."

o o o

"I'm having Layla withdrawals," Frank says the next morning when I pick up the phone, half asleep. "When can I see you?"

"Um," I say. *Have I not been sitting here with my thumb up my ass, waiting for you to give me the time of day?*

"Listen, I don't know about you, but I could use a little road trip. I'd like to take you skiing this weekend. Is that something you think you'd like to do? I mean, I know you're a big skier—"

"That sounds great," I say.

So he couldn't see me for a week after sleeping with me. So what? Don't I want a guy with a good work ethic? Isn't that the kind of man I want to settle down and have kids with?

Frank says we can stay with a college friend of his who lives up near Sugarbush, so it'll be low-key cashwise, which is good. My money situation is getting bad. I don't even have enough for a lift ticket, especially now that it costs over seventy bucks a day for the pleasure of skiing Vermont's crusty boilerplate. There are many things I don't want Frank to know, and my being broke is one of them. Pulling out a fresh MasterCard from the bottom of my underwear drawer, I decide this is as good a time as any to rack up some credit-card debt.

"There's only one hitch," Frank says. "We need a car."

"No problem," I say immediately, although it very well might be. I'm so invested in making sure this is the most extraordinary getaway ever that I offer to do something I'd prefer not to—ask Jamie if I can borrow hers.

The first thing she says is "He's taking you away for the weekend and he hasn't rented a car?"

"Right." *Good point.*

But Jamie is so in seventh heaven that she's delighted to be of service. Now that she's on the road to connubial bliss, she wants to do everything possible to facilitate my relationship with Frank. "You may absolutely borrow my car!" she says. "After driving Tom's car, I'm thinking of getting rid of it anyways."

"Tom's got a car, too?"

"A Beemer. It is so incredible. Those cars practically drive themselves, you know?"

"Yeah."

o o o

Jamie's four-year-old Jetta is a zippy car, and I love driving it. Love driving in general. Want Frank to see, in fact, what a good driver I am. Put myself in the driver's seat, as it were.

I pick him up with all his gear, and he comes around to my side, asking, "Mind if I drive?"

"Ah, no. Sure. Go ahead," I say, immediately berating myself for being such a pushover. So much for bowling him over with my Mario Andretti routine.

Frank seems to know what he's doing, which is a relief and, as far as I'm concerned, a major character enhancer. At Forty-second Street on the West Side Highway, he pulls out the one hitter, holds it in between his teeth, and says, "There's been a change of plans. We won't be staying with my friend after all." He doesn't explain why. "I've made a reservation for us at the Piney Lodge Chalet."

Is he going to pay for the motel? Or are we supposed to split it? Here goes my stomach again.

It's a long drive, and though he doesn't come right out and say it, I can tell Frank is underwhelmed with my CD selections. I think it's "Bat Out of Hell" that pushes him over the edge.

I'm singing all of the words, perfectly pitched, timed, and inflected, clearly enjoying myself way too much, when Frank says, "How about some Ween?"

"Okay," I say, "after this song, all right?"

The sirens are screamin' and the fires are howlin'
Way down in the valley tonight . . .

Frank keeps his bloodshot eyes on the road, and I become alarmed when he doesn't answer. Sometimes this is all it takes to put a man off. "Or even right now," I say, popping the Meatloaf CD out and putting the Ween in. Frank's face softens. Whatever makes him happy.

I'm hoping this weekend will break down some barriers, allow Frank and me to settle into a more familiar way of being together. I wish we could just skip this whole uncomfortable phase and move on to finishing each other's sentences.

We stop at a McDonald's, and I order a Filet-O-Fish meal with a "Caution Filling Is Hot!" apple pie. Frank has a Big Mac and supersizes the fries and milk shake.

"I don't think I've ever seen anyone eat one of those things," he says as the pimply-faced girl at the counter places individually wrapped items on the papered tray.

"The Filet-O-Fish?"

"Yeah."

"You should try one sometime."

"Maybe I will. And an apple pie, huh? You're really going all out."

This comment causes me to instinctively suck in my stomach and jam my hand in my front pocket to feel around for the twenty-dollar bill I've brought in case of emergencies. I hold the crumpled bill in my hand so Frank can see it. See that I'm no freeloader, that I am prepared to pay for both of our meals. The girl says, "That'll be thirteen-fifty."

Frank quickly hands her a twenty, saying, "I think I can handle this one."

He's acting sort of weird and distant, and it's affecting me badly. Even though he's paid for the Mickey D's, I get the distinct feeling he's trying to save his money. What happened to "Layla withdrawals"?

We arrive just after midnight. The Piney Lodge Chalet has big windows in the front, with the motel rooms spreading out like wings from its center. We tumble from the car like Cheech and Chong. It is cold and quiet—big fluffy snowflakes falling.

There is already a dusting of light snow on the ground and I kick it up with my hiking boots as we lug skis, boots, and bags from the trunk of the car into the motel. "The snow's going to be good tomorrow," I say.

"I can't wait," Frank says.

Relief sweeps over me. I think it's so cute that Frank can't wait. I picture a little boy all bundled up by his mother, red faced and excited to spend the whole day out in the snow never even noticing he's cold or fatigued. . . . It's the smoothest exchange we've had since the trip began and it helps dissipate the thundercloud I've pictured hovering over the Jetta like a cartoon.

By the time we're in the room getting ready for bed, there is only one thing bothering me. I'm wearing some lacy underwear I bought five years ago at Victoria's Secret, and never wore, which has secretly been itching the shit out of my inner thighs the whole drive up. I pour merlot into two plastic motel cups. I won't have to worry about *those* for too much longer.

Unzipping my Patagonia pile jacket, Frank carefully pulls my Gap turtleneck over my head, giving me a penetrating gaze. There is something weirdly staged about his actions. Like *This is what I'm supposed to look like when I'm seducing you. Never mind. He's adorable. . . . He can't wait to ski.*

When he's got me laid out flat on the bed, he begins kissing my neck and, surpassing my lacy underwear, arrives quickly at my feet. His hair is messy, and the expression on his lips is porn-perfect.

My God, is he going to suck on my toes?

I can only hope and pray that never having suffered from foot odor means my feet smell okay now. *Alright. Get yourself together. Toe-sucking is uninhibited, toe-sucking is sexy. For god's sake, just go with it, Layla. . . .* Frank brushes the tip of his thumb back and forth over my big toe, as though warming it for a tasty meal. Licking it like a lollipop, he puts it in his mouth, hollowing out his cheeks as he sucks. Moving down the line, he's taking it slow, doing his own version of "This Little Piggy."

Lying naked on top of the plasticky bedcover, I'm getting goose bumps from the chill. Frank looks stupid sucking on my toes. And worse, I can't convince myself he enjoys it. I should be lost in the moment, but as with our last sexual encounter, I am not at ease and become even less so when Frank pulls out a pair of handcuffs and says, "Have you been a bad girl?"

I laugh, hoping he can't see the whites of my eyes, hoping I look game. "Oh yes," I say, trying to sound convincing, "a very bad girl."

"Here," he says, "put your hands behind your back."

Isn't it a little early in the game for handcuffs? Isn't this supposed to be the sort of thing you discuss ahead of time?

"Is this about Meatloaf?" I ask, hoping to break the ice. The last thing I want him to know is that I've never done this before. I want him to think of me as a woman of the world, a lady of experience.

But Frank's not laughing. His eyes are glazed, and he's in his own little world.

I am propped up on my knees, hoping I don't face-plant it into the cheesy wooded-glen watercolor on the wall, my hands handcuffed behind me. I don't feel like a woman of the world or a lady. I feel silly and uncomfortable, but Frank is turned on, so I pretend to be, too.

If Frank notices I'm not having as much fun as he is, he doesn't show it. He moves me around, lifting me up, placing me on my side, holding me forward and back, lifting my legs, propping up my ass while my face is squashed into the pillow.

So this is what getting fucked six ways from Sunday is like. After fifteen minutes, I start to feel like a blow-up doll. I try to think of ways to let myself go, but I'm totally devoid of plausible fantasies. Chalking it up to what must certainly be a hidden frigidity that's chosen to unveil itself at this critical moment, I go numb and wait for him to finish.

The handcuffs are too tight and leave a deep red mark around my wrists. Frank is all sweetness afterward, kissing the marks and rubbing them gently, asking, "Do they hurt?" They don't hurt, but for some reason, I still feel like crying. I'm not frightened, exactly. More ill at ease. A Freudian shrink once told me about another patient of his who fancied himself a sadist. Evidently, he could take one look at a girl and know whether she was into being punished. "That is an extreme example," the shrink said, "but you take my point?"

I did. It was all the stuff about secretly wanting to sleep with my father that I seriously questioned.

What I say I want is true love, just like every other human being on the planet. I want men on their knees holding little blue Tiffany's boxes. So why am I here in this two-bit motel getting handcuffed by Frank?

The shrink would say, tonguing the end of his unlit pipe (he had an oral fixation and was trying to give up smoking), "There must be something about it that you like."

If I were giving advice to another girl, I'd tell her to walk out the door and never look back. But things aren't so clear-cut when they're happening to you. There are various possibilities for Frank's behavior: A) He feels weak, insecure, and afraid, and tying women up gives him a sense—if only for a minute—that he's in control (inspires sticky pity, warm affection). B) He doesn't give a shit about me and has nothing to lose (pisses me off). C) He likes me and hopes I enjoy being tied up every now and again (wishful thinking shouldn't be condemned). D) It has nothing whatsoever to do with me, and if it weren't me, it would be somebody else (too hard to swallow). E) This is all just a big joke—ha! ha!

o o o

I do not sleep well. In the morning, I rub the goo out of my eyes while arranging the small round Maxwell House diskette in the motel coffeepot. Uncorking the merlot, I take a swig. Frank sits up in bed like a pasha and lights his one hitter. We are a pair of sorry asses, but in this moment it feels like wildness, it feels like the movies.

Actually, I'm just preparing myself. Some people say that alcohol's for cowards, but I think there's a damn good reason why they call it courage. I intend to roll Frank up and smoke him on the slopes today, but I've got a little performance anxiety. Frank, on the other hand, does not appear to be suffering any discomfort whatsoever.

I tell him I'm going to the lobby to get some local maps and information, then frantically run down the carpeted hallway that smells of stale cigarette smoke in search of a bathroom.

When I get back to the room twenty minutes later, Frank is sitting on the edge of the bed watching cartoons. He is dressed in nonfunctional skiwear—baggy army fatigues, a cotton turtleneck, and a denim jacket. "Did you find any?" he asks.

"Any what?" I respond.

"Maps," he says.

"Oh, right, maps. No, they didn't have any." And then, to diffuse the situation, "Aren't you going to be cold?"

"Nah," he says, not taking his eyes from the television, absentmindedly scratching his stubble with the tips of his fingers.

This devil-may-care attitude about being properly dressed is a major strike against him on so many different levels. Anyone who knows anything about the outdoors knows that you must always be prepared for the worst. In the wild, you are quickly disabused of the notion that skiing in jeans or army fatigues is anywhere close to cool, that cotton is anything more than the devil's fabric. Layers! And lots of them, in fabrics not known to nature. If you become lost on the mountain, these will save your life, wicking out the cold, clammy moisture that will eventually contribute to your dying an extremely slow (but, from what I've heard, not altogether unpleasant) death.

I smugly begin my vestments. Starting with polypropylene long-underwear tops and bottoms, I layer myself with manmade fabrics until I'm ready for the Gore-Tex icing—a rugged pair of overalls with reinforced butt and knees and a jacket with pit zips and powder band.

"You look official," Frank says.

Little does he know. A person cannot ski every day for three seasons running and not be halfway decent. I know I look official. I *am* official, handcuff boy!

As we park in the lot at Sugarbush, I hand Frank my credit card and pray he doesn't use it to buy tickets. It does briefly cross my mind that though he invited me on this ski weekend, the key ingredient he was supposed to provide—i.e., free lodging—has already fallen through. If I take care of transportation and lift tickets, I am effectively on my way to paying for the whole damn excursion. Well, he did spring for the Mickey D's.

The sun is shining, and the temperature is a crisp 25 degrees. There was a major dump two days ago, so the snow in the trees and ungroomed sections is still powdery. Frank lights up the one hitter in the chair lift, but I demur. He is already starting to shiver. Zipping up the Mountain Hardwear and pulling high my gator, I lower my goggles so that my entire face is protected. *Go ahead. Get good and high.*

I snowplow as we exit the lift. I don't want to give away anything too soon. From Frank's first move, I can see he's unsteady—legs straight, ankles and shoulders stiff, poles sticking out at angles that suggest crutch use. What he lacks in technique, I soon discover, he makes up for in speed. Shooting ahead of me, he twists his shoulders to initiate turns, stiffly yanks the uphill ski around for lack of proper weighting.

I watch from the top of the pitch as he slides in high-speed slow motion, one ski falling behind and to the side, so that he spins backward in one balletic move, and KABLOOEY!

A few people on the chair call, "Are you okay?" A group of teenagers begins cheering. Skiing down to him, I pick up the released ski thirty yards up the mountain, hat (twenty-one), goggles (twenty), and pole (ten). When I get to Frank, he's flustered and angry with himself. "I didn't see that coming," he says.

"Maybe you need to warm up a little?" I suggest.

"Yeah."

Somewhere toward the last pitch of the mountain, he stops to watch me. I breathe deeply, and I make my brain go blank. Effectively putting the kibosh on the greatest impediment all skiers must face—fear. Roll 'em. I point my tips down a section of soft, fluffy moguls. My knees jam like an accordion—bang, bang, bang, oof, oof, oof. I'm in the rhythm, picking up controlled speed, eyes up, poles impaling, popping a wide spread eagle off the final bump. I do not fuck up. I do not let myself down. I show Frank what I'm made of. Who is that Mistress of the Mountain? That female banshee on boards? Let people speak of the thrill, fresh air, and rigorous exercise that skiing affords them. For Layla Mitchner, skiing is a hopeful reminder that there are some things in this world she knows, without a doubt, she does well.

Pulling a Suzy Chapstick, I shoosh to a stop next to Frank. He's crouched down, messing with his boot buckle. He missed the matinée.

The day is warming up. I remove my hat and hang my goggles around my neck so that my head can breathe. Frank and I are standing in line for the quad when, alternating with an opposing line, I see someone who looks awfully familiar. She's dressed more for ballet than skiing, her shiny beige stretch pants molding themselves to that sorry excuse for an ass, the matching beige square-stitch down fur-trimmed jacket hugging her skinny waist. It's Lucinda. And to her left, standing tall in skiwear almost identical to mine, is Dick Davenport.

Lucinda's nattering on about something while Dick stares in my direction. The two of us recognize each other at approximately the same moment. "Layla?" he asks.

"Dick!" Why I'm so happy to see Dick Davenport, I cannot say. Maybe because this weekend has been so harrowing that any familiar face is welcome. I feel like I've run into a long-lost friend.

"What are you doing here?" he asks.

"Same thing you are," I say, smiling, wondering if maybe I should reach forward and hug him.

"You remember Lucinda?"

"Yeah, hi. Good to see you again. This is Frank," I say. The rising temperature has melted all of the snow accumulated on Frank's person—his soaked army fatigues hang low on his haunches, and the smell of wet wool emanates from him in soggy whiffs. He looks miserable.

"Nice to meet you, Frank," Dick says. "This is Lucinda."

"Hi," Lucinda says, all curt bitchiness.

"Good to see you!" Dick looks almost as relieved as I am. Lucinda begins arranging her headband and Gucci sunglasses so that her hair can be on perfect display. She reaches into her jacket pocket and pulls out—can it be?—a compact mirror and begins applying lipstick. I become aware, almost immediately, of how unfeminine I look, how Muppetlike my outgrown short hair is.

Two from that side, two from this—alternating—it looks like we're going to end up on the same chair. Dick and I get in the middle, while Frank and Lucinda move to the outside. The chair comes, and Lucinda sits daintily before scuffling with her pole. "Oh, Dick!" she whines, "my pole! My pole!"

"It's okay, Luce, we'll get it on our next run."

"But I can't ski with one pole!"

"I'll give you one of mine."

This quiets her down.

"So you're a skier, I see," Dick says to me.

I nod, pressing my lips together in confirmation.

"Whatever happened to you at that party? You sort of disappeared."

"Yeah. You know what they say, if you can't stand the heat . . ."

"You seemed to be handling the situation like a pro."

"Yeah, well."

"Your mother's quite a piece of work."

"Mmm."

"Hey, what do you say we all ski a run together?"

Lucinda's expression resembles the villain's in a cartoon: *Drat, foiled again!* Frank looks upset about not being able to light up.

"Sounds good," I say.

Dick surprises me when he says, "Billy tells me you used to instruct out West?"

"True," I say.

"Maybe you can give Lucinda a few pointers. She doesn't like to listen to me."

"He's been trying to stick me in a lesson all day," Lucinda says.

"Lessons can be helpful," I offer.

"Not if you already know how to ski," she says, giving me death darts.

Frank says, "Lessons, shmessions. Just have fun."

At the top, Lucinda inches off the chair in a snowplow, and Dick stays by her side, offering a hand of support and then giving her his pole.

We'll be sticking to an easy intermediate run. Dick and I stand together and watch as our paramours make their way down—Lucinda moving slow and cautious, Frank screaming down like hell on skis, a master of disaster.

"After you," Dick says, and I shove off, skiing down past Lucinda to where Frank is waiting for us. I can see Dick at the top of the fall line, his eyes on Lucinda, waiting to see if she'll need his help. And then he takes off, carving large, fast GS turns, skiing like a racer. *Well, surprise, surprise. So he's not just a suit . . .*

Lucinda reaches us just before Dick. And Frank says something to Dick that I've been waiting all day for him to say to me: "Hey, you're good."

"Thanks," Dick says.

"He's been skiing all his life," Lucinda adds.

o o o

My dream of steak *au poivre* with crispy *frites* in a homey inn-type place is a top priority. I'm craving a good meal with a nice bottle of wine, and I'm willing to go further into debt to get it. I'm still clinging to my memories of three weeks ago, of Frank and me dreamily sucking the blood out of steaks at 1492. But when I suggest someplace nice to Frank that evening, he says, "I was sort of thinking about ordering a pizza or something."

A pizza or something? I am crushed beyond all reasonable measure. "Come on," I say, growing desperate, "my treat."

Back in the steamy motel bathroom, I can hear Frank talking in low tones on his cell phone while I lotion up after my
shower. Rifling through my dop kit, I find a small cloth pouch
of makeup. I've brought along a pair of tight, hip-hugger jeans
as well as a see-through black shirt and bra. Not exactly comfort clothes, not completely me, they are new purchases. I
apply foundation, blush, lipstick, and mascara, and struggle
into the tight clothes. I think I've lost weight. I think I can carry
it off. I want Frank's jaw to drop—for him to be jolted from *Behind the Music* and fall from the bed, frothing at the mouth.

It would appear, however, that Aerosmith is far too engross-
ing. Walking over to the window, I crack it and seductively light
a cigarette. *Look at me, look at me, look at me* . . .

Peeling his eyes away from the TV for a moment, he asks,
"Are you wearing makeup?" Like he's my mother and I'm
twelve and he wishes I weren't. Then, "Aren't you going to be
uncomfortable in that outfit?"

Oh my.

The Steak Pub is a dark, woody affair with a large salad bar. We
both order $8 hurricanes from the special drinks card, at which
point Frank proceeds to tick off items from the menu like some
high roller in Vegas. "Let's see, I'll have the stuffed mush-
rooms, shrimp cocktail, beef tenderloin, think they'd have
some of that Béarnaise sauce on the side? Salad bar. . . . I'll
take the all-you-can-eat salad bar, actually, for what is it—two
dollars extra? That okay with you, Layla?"

I'm adding up prices in my head—mushroom caps $8.95,
shrimp cocktail $11.95, tenderloin $25.95! Having never used
this card before, I have no idea if it's even going to work, but I

nod enthusiastically and say, "Of course!" If I have to do dishes, I have to do dishes. Or we could pull a chew-and-screw. I begin to hate Frank for putting me in this situation, for being cheap, for allowing a woman—whom he may but most likely may not care about—to pay for his dinner.

I will not be denied my steak. I order the cheapest cut, with no appetizer or salad bar, just the baked potato and side vegetable—sautéed zucchini—that come with the dish.

When the meal arrives, my steak is tough. I chew it slowly, trying to break it down, thinking I could always feign choking. Frank gets up from the table again and again for more crusty bread and extra vegetables with blue-cheese dressing. "This was a great idea," he says at one point. Unfortunately, I'm too nervous about my card not going through to enjoy myself. The closer we get to dessert, the more fidgety I become.

Mud pie and an Irish coffee for Frank, nothing for me. Even though all I want to do is stick my whole face in an ice-cream sundae.

Getting up to use the ladies' room, I decide to stop at the waitron station and deal with the bill away from the table. The MasterCard is slid, and I wait, holding my breath, for the little machine to start making clicking noises. Watching the waitress wiggle the pen between her first and second fingers nearly pushes my racing heart over the edge. I stand in silence waiting, waiting, waiting. She looks up at me and asks, "Do you have another card?"

"No," I say. And then, trying to sound confident, "This one should work."

"Well, sometimes we have problems with this machine. Let me try running it through again."

Please work. Puleeeeeeese.

"Layla?"

The voice is familiar. The flash of recognition prickles my cheeks. "Dick."

"Did you two enjoy your meal?"

"Oh, yeah," I say, trying to sound enthusiastic, "it was delicious." The waitress could care less whether or not I enjoyed anything, because my card is not going through.

Dick stands there. I can't tell whether he's aghast that my card's not going through or that I'm paying for dinner. Pulling me aside, he asks, "Are you having trouble? I can lend you cash if for some reason your card's not working."

He sounds like my father, who, come to think of it, I wish were here right now. I am horrified and humiliated but try to remain calm. "Oh, no, it's okay. I've got cash, too," I say, reaching around to my back pocket for a nonexistent wallet.

Things are starting to get critical when the music from the machine begins. I'm so relieved that, for the second time that day, I feel like hugging Dick, who smiles and says, "Stupid machines." And then, "You look pretty tonight. I almost didn't recognize you."

"I'd be hard to miss with these headlights." *What did I just say?*

"You got that right," he says, laughing good-naturedly. Then, changing the subject like a gentleman, he asks, "What's good here?"

"The steak is pretty good," I say. "You should go for the tenderloin."

"Is that your official answer?" he asks, leaning in toward me like Regis Philbin.

"That is my professional advice," I reply.

"Ah, but you're just a *plebe* . . . in your own words, of course."

How the hell did he remember that? "Yeah, well," I say, looking down at my shoes.

"I'm just joking, you know. I took some friends to Tacoma after Billy's party."

"You did?"

"The salad was the best thing on the menu."

This makes me way happier than it should. "Did you have the Caesar or the mixed greens with Gorgonzola, pear, and toasted walnuts?"

"Both," he says, looking at me intensely.

Very big blue eyes.

"Well, I should be getting back," he says, almost apologetically, but he doesn't move. Instead, we stand there in silence for a couple of seconds. Then, putting his hand on my arm, he says, "It was great running into you."

"Likewise," I say.

As he turns to walk back toward his table, I notice he's got on worn Levi's that hang beautifully from what appears to be an extremely nice set of haunches. He looks more crunchy than preppy tonight. *Versatile.*

When I get back from the bathroom, there is a bucket on our table, with a bottle of champagne propped to the side and two flutes half filled with bubbly.

"What's all this?" I say, smiling at Frank, the horror and tension of the weekend dissolving.

"Our friend Dick sent it over," Frank says magnanimously.

"Dick?" I ask, confused.

"Don't look at me," Frank says, shrugging. "There's a note

on a napkin here." He holds it limply between thumb and forefinger.

In neat block letters it says, *Here's that refill I promised you.
Enjoy!*

I didn't realize how shitty I felt about the entire weekend
until just now. My nose is getting stuffy, and my eyes are starting to water.

"Cheers!" Frank says, looking like things keep getting better and better.

Bucking up, I try to smile as I hold up my glass and say, "Le-
chaim." Too bad it took Dick Davenport to show me just how
low I've sunk.

o o o

I have great hopes for West 12th, if only because the chef, Laurie, is a woman and I figure we'll have that in common. The
restaurant is empty at six on a Wednesday night. In its former
life, it was more mod and "not as busy." It still looks not as
busy to me, although someone has put a lot of moolah into the
place to give it that faux country charm. There are little bundles
of dried flowers in the center of each table, tasteful wrought-
iron candlesticks with old-time wax catchers and honeycomb
candles. The walls are brick and the floors wide-plank pine.

Laurie is in the kitchen getting her mise en place in order.
Besides the dishwasher and prep guy, she's the only one working. There's a cutting board with chopped parsley and several
plastic containers containing items like sliced scallion, crumbled egg, chopped shallots, rectangles of roasted pepper, and
crumbled blue cheese. Nothing new here. Laurie is going

through each, sticking her nose in, sampling little bits to see what can be saved. She is a large woman, on the thin side of fat, with bushy light brown curls. There are bunches of plastic wrap scattered on one section of counter, flour with a ball of dough on another. I have no idea how she expects to be ready for service.

"Come in, come in!" she says when she sees me standing at the door. "You're Layla?"

"Yeah, hi, nice to meet you," I say, offering my hand, which I'm really hoping she refuses to shake. Wiping her oil-stained hands on a kitchen towel hanging from the top of her apron, she grabs my hand in hers, which is plump, warm, and slimy.

The dishwasher is trimming and washing piles of kale, while the prep cook dices carrots, onion, and celery. Laurie gestures toward him and says, "Meet Pedro and Felipe."

"Is it just the three of you?" I ask.

"You bet," she says, turning to her containers and continuing her work. "Sorry, do you mind? I've got to have this stuff ready in half an hour. We only have two tables on the books so far, but you've got to be ready for walk-ins. I've still got to get that bread in the oven. Oh, shit! Pedro, why don't you drop the kale for a minute and get that dough on a tray."

"Is this a bad time?" It's a rhetorical question. I don't know why she told me to come at this hour. Unless she was positive it wouldn't be busy. Which, at this early point in the evening, it doesn't seem to be.

"No, no problem. I wanted you to get a sense of what it was like here during service. Gustav tells me you worked the garde-manger at Tacoma?"

"Yeah, and the Eagle Café, and Le Diamond in France."

"You went to cooking school?"

"The Cordon Bleu."

"Wow, that's great." She's trimming the ends off a bunch of scallions. After, she begins to slice them two at a time, slowly. Her knife work is not confident.

An order for one house salad and one salmon terrine comes in. Laurie is in the middle of doing three other things, but she stops, runs to the large metallic fridge, pulls out a metal terrine dish, and yells, "Quick, Pedro! A pan and some hot water!" Plunking it into the warm water, she turns to her large silver bowl, throws in a bunch of mesclun greens, some crumbled old egg, blue cheese, diced tomatoes, cucumber, salt, pepper. "Shit, I haven't made the vinaigrette!"

Grabbing another bowl from the shelf, I move quickly to the fridge, find the mustard, put two tablespoons into the bowl along with some red-wine vinegar, salt, and pepper, and begin whisking it rapidly, then slowly, pouring in the olive oil. I can see Laurie out of the corner of my eye, unmolding the salmon terrine, smoothing it out on the edges with her filthy fingers, licking them as she goes. I would not want to be on the receiving end of that.

Hoping to save the salad eater from a similar fate, I head for the sink, where Pedro of the white, mushy, waterlogged fingers politely lets me through to scrub my hands with dishwashing liquid. Back to the salad. Spooning the vinaigrette over the greens, I thrust my hands in and toss. Pedro has set a plate down on the floured counter next to me. Grabbing a bunch of mesclun with both hands, I place it deftly in the middle of the plate, scrunch and twist Tacoma-style, strategically placing cucumber and tomato in and among the lettuce.

"Nice job!" Laurie calls. A rectangular slice of salmon rests innocently on a white plate, with sprigs of chervil and squiggles of dill cream to garnish.

Laurie informs me that my starting salary will be $75 a day, as opposed to the $100 I was making at Tacoma. Can beggars afford to be choosers? Here is a situation where help is clearly needed, but instead of seeing this as an opportunity to rise up, assert myself, and help the frazzled Laurie whip the place into shape, I am left limp and unmotivated. I suppose you could even say depressed. Well, there is something depressing about West 12th. It reeks of failure. Too much money on the decor, not enough on the kitchen staff. I decide to be a choosy beggar. It may be the wrong decision, but I just can't face that little faux-country excuse for a restaurant. I'm not sure I can face any restaurant at this stage of the game.

o o o

"I'm so sorry, Lay, I didn't know who else to call." It's ten P.M. and Dina's crying from the bar phone at Tacoma.

"Shhh," I say, trying to calm her, "take a couple of breaths and tell me what's wrong."

"Can you meet me after my shift? Shit, I don't know if I'll even be able to make it that long."

"It's okay," I say, "you can hold it together. I'll meet you wherever you want."

"Can you come here?"

I really, really don't want to set foot in Tacoma ever again, but I say, "What time?"

"Two o'clock?"

"I'll be there."

John, the night manager, is going through the till with Dina when I walk in. The bar is wiped clean, dark and empty. John lifts up the end piece of the bar, walks through, and lowers it. "Good night," he says, referring to the profits.

"One of my best yet," Dina confirms.

"Hey, Layla, didn't think I'd see you back here so soon," John says.

"Neither did I."

"Well, you two ladies can close up, I take it?"

"No problem," Dina says, waving him out the door. Blowing out a huge sigh, she asks, "What can I get for you?"

"How about a Baileys."

"Good choice. You want rocks?"

"Yeah."

Pulling two tumblers from under the bar, she fills them with ice and pours the Baileys up to the rim. She clinks her glass on mine. We swirl and sip. The sweet, creamy taste registers as heaven. "Well," she says, staring at her drink.

"What's going on?"

Walking from behind the bar, she sits slumped on the stool next to mine, her sun tattoo slacking in the small ripples of stomach skin. When she finally looks up at me, she is crying. "Fucking Stan," she says, shaking her head. "That fucking ass-hole's been screwing one of the makeup girls."

"Shit." Not too eloquent, I know, but sometimes the only way to respond to this type of information. "I always thought things were so good between you."

"They were so good! They *were*. I mean, we were the perfect couple. I felt so comfortable with him, you know? He adored me! *Adored* me!" I take a sip of my drink, but Dina's crying too hard to drink hers, the ice melting, becoming watery on the top. "She's twenty-five, and he says he won't stop seeing her. He's obsessed with her, obsessed with fucking her."

"Shit."

"I mean, how immature do you have to be? To throw everything away just because you like fucking someone?"

"People can be pretty stupid sometimes," I say, wary of making too many disparaging remarks about Stan lest they reunite.

"And I'm turning thirty-nine this week, did you know that? Thirty-fucking-*nine*! So much for the kid thing."

"I thought you didn't care about having kids."

"So did I." She's shaking, and I'm standing next to her, hugging her, her head resting on my shoulder.

"It's going to be okay," I say.

"I suggested we go and see someone, like a counselor or something. Shit, a *counselor*. It just goes to show how low I've sunk. I've never had anything but scorn and ridicule for counselors and shrinks or whatever, and now I'm, like, *begging* him, I am *down* on my *hands* and *knees* . . ."

"And?"

"He says he'll go with me, but he won't stop fucking her."

"That's kind of hard to work with."

"How am I supposed to sit there and discuss our relationship with someone who adamantly refuses to stop fucking this other little cunt?"

"I think the cessation of fucking would be a hopeful sign."

Dina laughs despite herself, then angrily chants, "Fuck him, fuck him, fuck *hiiiim*." She's shaking her head, leaning over the bar, searching for her cigarettes.

"I got it," I say, pulling a pack out of my jacket, taking two out, lighting them, and handing her one.

"By the way, whatever happened with the babe at the Hogs?" I shrug.

"Did you two hit it off?"

"Oh yeah," I say, "but things have unraveled pretty quickly."

"You two got together, then?" she asks, interested, relieved to discuss someone else's shitty love luck.

"Yup."

"So what's going on?"

"I'm not exactly sure," I say, trying not to let on what a disaster the whole thing has been. "I've been kind of obsessed. I think he's sort of unavailable, though."

"Is he seeing someone else?" Dina asks hopefully.

"I don't know. I don't think so," I say, but now that she's mentioned it, it would explain a few things.

"Hm. Sometimes it can be tougher when there isn't someone else. Then it's just like he's not into *you*."

I would be offended by this if I didn't agree with her. "Yeah, that makes it almost harder to swallow."

"Well, give it some time."

"He's also sort of into S&M," I say, deciding to come partially clean.

"*What?*" she screams, a shocked smile on her face.

I backpedal. "Nothing too extreme, just handcuffs, satin ties, stuff like that."

"Did he hurt you? I will fucking rip that guy's balls off—"

"Not really. It's just sort of weird, you know? We still don't really know each other that well."

"Well, fuck that! I mean, you can do what you want when you

trust someone and feel comfortable with him and it's mutual. Was it mutual?"

"Well, I didn't exactly object. I didn't want him to think I was a dweeb."

"So he tied you up, and now he's blowing you off?"

"I don't know. We went to Vermont last weekend, and it kind of sucked."

"Well, *yeah*," she says, "it's not like he's working that hard at building up your trust if he's pulling shit with handcuffs already. Has he called?"

"Negative." I'm not even going to bring up the fact that I ended up putting the whole weekend on my credit card.

"What an asshole."

"*I'm* the one that feels like an asshole," I say.

"Whatever you do, don't call him. Sometimes, with guys, if they think you could give a shit, they really can't take it. Not that I'm suggesting he's worth the time of day."

"Is that the tactic you're pulling with Stan?"

"He knows me too well. Knows I'm crushed already."

"But maybe if he thought you were moving on, like you have someone else, too."

"Layla, I'm a thirty-eight-year-old bartender. Who'd want me? At my age, men will be hightailing it as soon as they hear that ticking getting closer." She looks into her glass as though she will find the answer to the riddle that is her life.

I cannot believe Dina, one of the hottest women I know, could think men won't find her attractive anymore. I say, "What, Stan dumps you, and all of a sudden you're going to lose your feminine magnetism? Men can't resist you."

"When I was *taken*, men couldn't resist me," she corrects. "Now you'll see. They can smell desperation a mile away."

"Did you ever freeze those eggs?" I ask hopefully.

She doesn't say anything, and it appears I've crossed some line. I wonder if she's about to start crying all over again. When she looks up at me, though, her eyes are dancing, her sad face widening into a smile. "Yeah," she says. "You better fucking believe I did."

○ ○ ○

Despite the fact that I have never gotten a job from my résumé, I decide to set up my old college computer and go through the sickening motions of updating. With this testament of amateurish instability before me, I scrutinize the document the way I imagine a potential employer might, and conclude that they would conclude I'm a flake. Video production? Paralegal? Ski instructor? Cocktail waitress? Cook? This is not a well-balanced person, a person who sticks to things and, with hard work and perseverance, acquires skills! Moves up the ladder! Careerbuilds! As I pick apart my résumé for the first time in years, it becomes clear to me that I am a jack-of-all-trades, master of none. I am twenty-eight years old, have chosen cooking as my profession, and will be damned if I'm going to abandon it. I have to make it work, no matter how much I've grown to hate every minute in a professional kitchen.

Playing up cooking school, trilinguality, travel, and adding a few restaurants to my list of places worked, I manage to fill a whole page with nothing but cooking-related jobs. I was not a waitress and ski instructor but a grill cook at the Cottonwood Lodge in Alta, Utah, not a paralegal but an executive dining room sauté cook at Bartle, Jankman and Phipps. I produced food shows with Poker Productions (true).

Addressing it to the Cooking Channel, I lick the envelope, place a stamp in the right-hand corner, and drop it in a mailbox.

o o o

Time is running out. Jamie is moving. I have no money and am going deeper into credit-card debt (the worst kind!) by the day. But never mind all that. What I need, I decide, is a place of my own.

Gustav lives in Greenpoint and says I can find a place out there for the same price I was paying to split the place with Jamie. This sounds good to me. Since moving to California's no longer on my agenda, moving across the river will be the next best thing. Brooklyn, the new frontier! This isn't quite true. Brooklyn was the new frontier, say, fifteen years ago. Now you can't just put down a stake and park your wagon. You need to consider less accessible (cheaper) neighborhoods, like Greenpoint, Clinton Hill, and Long Island City, which is technically Queens.

I scour *The Village Voice* on Tuesday night and the Sunday *Times* on Saturday, imagining in snapshot every "cozy garden studio" and "charming, sunny one-bedroom." How much happier I will be in a new, more neighborhoody neighborhood, where the local butcher knows my name and I can have tag sales on my front stoop. It will be nothing like cold, impersonal Manhattan, where no one knows you and no one cares. Especially Frank. I'm ready for change, a little small-town human interaction.

Gabbing with me on the phone, Billy says, "Do not tell me you're moving to Brooklyn."

"I'm looking," I say.

"Looking to leave the greatest city in the world?"

"It's just across the river."

"It might as well be Timbuktu! I'll never see you now."

"You haven't seen me in almost a month anyways, and we live on the same side of the island."

"Miguel," he says, sighing.

"Is it love?"

"I'm afraid I'm completely dick-whipped."

"I hope it doesn't hurt."

"Honey, you don't even want to know. . . . Well, you're braver than I am. I vowed when I moved here that I was coming to live in Manhattan, and that's where I'm stayin'." He sounds like Barbara Stanwyck in a Western.

"I can't afford it."

"Oh, don't give me that crap. Ask Julia to help you."

"No."

"Well . . ." I can tell he doesn't want to say what he's about to say, but he can't resist. "Didn't your father leave you anything?"

"It's gone."

"What do you mean, it's gone?"

"I mean, he only left me enough for graduate school, and I've spent it."

"The man was a frickin' millionaire!"

I like to forget about this whenever possible. It's not until Billy brings it up that I sink into a mire of self-pity, where I become overwhelmed by how cruel and unusually I've been punished by parents who never loved me. "I know," I say.

"So where's all the dough?"

"I don't know, he never discussed it with me. I assume my mother got some in the divorce, and his girlfriend got the rest."

"That sucks."

"I don't want his money."

"Yes, you do."

"No, I don't."

"Sweetheart, Angus Mitchner would not want this, I'm sure of it."

"You're making it sound like I'm going to be living on the street, Billy. Shit. It's Brooklyn! It's very nice there."

"Well, I hope you're at least looking in the Heights."

"I can't afford the Heights."

"The farther away you go, the less your friends will visit," he sings.

"I guess I'll know who my friends are, then."

"So where *can* you afford to move, Mary Poppins?"

"I'm looking into Greenpoint."

"*GUNPOINT?*"

"That's cute."

"The last time I was in *Gunpoint*, Layla, I almost didn't make it out alive."

"It's a safe Polish neighborhood."

"*Whatever*..."

"It'll be a new experience."

"That's putting it mildly. I hope you've got some Mace or some of that red-pepper spray."

Wanting to change the subject, I say, "Guess who I ran into last weekend at Sugarbush?"

"Dick Davenport."

"How did you know?"

"He told me. And, I have to say, I am very disappointed in you."

"What now?"

"He said you were there with some guy."

"Yeah, he was there with some girl."

"Well, if you hadn't run screaming into the night from my party, that whole thing with Lucinda might not have had a chance to flourish."

This is not fair. I've been stewing over that party ever since it happened—that Dick and I didn't hit it off, that Julia showed, that I got stuck shucking oysters in the kitchen all night. "Billy, I hate to break the news to you, but Dick is not my type, and I really don't think I'm his."

"He said you were a really good skier."

"He did?"

"Yes."

"Huh."

"*Yeah*, huh."

"He's a pretty good skier himself."

"So I'd have to gather, seeing as how *all of the* Davenports grew up on skis."

"You are such a snob."

"Don't pretend you grew up in some ghetto. I'm not going to lump you in with the poor huddled masses yet."

"Well, you better *start* lumping, because I may have grown up with champagne tastes, but I'm getting closer and closer to Miller Time every day."

"That makes no sense, but never mind. Who, may I ask, was the guy?"

"It's over."

"I didn't even know it had begun!"

"I had high hopes. To tell you the truth, I'm kind of upset about the whole thing."

"Who ditched whom," Billy asks, sounding like a census worker.

"I guess it was kind of mutual. He sort of blew me off, and I responded in kind."

"What do you mean, sort of blew you off?"

"You know, when you just get that feeling—that someone's not available? Like when you make an effort to put on a little makeup and wear something sexy and their reaction is not 'Wow! You look amazing!' but all disappointed, like, 'You're wearing makeup,' as if it's the least flattering thing in the world?"

"You put on makeup and something sexy for this turkey? You didn't put on makeup and something sexy for Dick."

"Yeah, well."

"And he didn't appreciate it?"

"He made me feel ashamed. That's the last time I'll be getting dressed up for a man for a while."

"Now, hold on a second. You do realize that if you fell for this guy, there's probably something fundamentally wrong with him. Dick didn't seem too impressed."

"Dick mentioned Frank?"

"Frank? *Frank?* The guy sounds like a plumber."

"He's not a plumber," I say defensively, although I don't know why. "He's a Renaissance man."

"Oh, brother."

"He's not for everyone."

"Can I be blunt?" Billy asks, his voice getting heated.

"When have you ever had to ask?"

"You know I care about you, right?"

"If you say so."

"Well, as your friend, I need to tell you—you have been through enough dead-end romances with fuck-ups to realize that no one you've ever dated has been for everyone. You've got a knack for pickin' the bad pickles."

"Not to put too fine a point on it."

"Was that bad?"

"No. You're right.

"I'm not saying I'm Mr. Relationship."

"I hope not."

"But I'm gay. It's expected. Don't you ever think of settling down with someone?"

The hair follicles in the back of my head have started to tingle, because yes, of course I think about it. I think about it a lot. But I say, "Occasionally."

"You better think of it more than occasionally, 'cause you're not gettin' any younger, lady friend."

"Thanks for the news flash."

"You're welcome."

"Good-bye."

"No, wait! Don't hang up. . . . I'm just upset that it didn't work out for you with Dick."

"It wouldn't be the first time."

"Listen, if you need to make some cash, my aunt Dory is always looking for someone to cater her parties. Can I assume you're interested?"

"That would be great," I say, even though the thought of catering some snooty society lady's party scares the shit out of me.

"I'll give her a call."

"By the way, do you have Dick's address? I want to write him a thank-you note."

"For what?"

"He sent over a bottle of Dom last weekend."

"*Classy*," Billy says. "I hope the plumber appreciated it."

"I appreciated it."

"There may be hope for you yet."

o o o

The whole Frank debacle puts me in an ugly and unfortunate state of mind. As much of an insecure control freak as I've diagnosed him as being, that he's a prick and I'm well rid of him ought to be perfectly clear to me by now.

I simply cannot believe I've been used and discarded in such a fashion. I am frankly wounded that he hasn't called since we got back to New York. And this, along with feeling like a total reject, is something I need to get to the bottom of. I go over and over in my head what I did wrong. Did I pay for too much? Seem too eager? Turn him off sexually? Was I not game enough with the handcuffs? Too assertive? Overpowering? Not ladylike enough? Well, screw him anyway. Oh, I forgot, I can't screw him because he probably doesn't care if he ever screws me again!

During this week, I eat very little, not intentionally but because my attraction to food is on hiatus. Even ice cream. The weight is dropping off. I'm eating one grilled-cheese sandwich a day, with the occasional avocado and grapefruit thrown in for good measure. This isn't a diet. I'm getting thinner, but I can't even enjoy it because I'm too obsessed with why Frank doesn't want me. There's no way around it—rejection blows.

Dina calls a couple of times a day, usually crying out of control. One night, while we're having dinner at Jean Claude (after polishing off a bottle and a half of wine), and are both so sad neither of us even wants to talk, I tell her this: "You need to get laid." Which is the same advice I might consider giving myself right about now.

She says, "Really? You think so?"

I say, "Nothing serious, just pick up one of the young cuties who frequent your bar, take him home, and fuck his brains out."

"That might give me something else to focus on besides the bad porno reruns I've got going in my head, starring Stan and his makeup bitch."

"Have you seen her?"

"Unfortunately, yes."

"Is she cute?"

"You could say that, yeah."

"She's probably really dumb."

"Not really. She graduated from Barnard two years ago."

"How do you know that?"

"Because Stan's been illuminating the nature of their relationship so that I'll be able to understand why he can't stop fucking her. It's not just physical, he says. They've got this intellectual *soul* connection as well."

"He sounds like the Marquis de Sade."

"If I didn't love him so much, I'd probably get a lot of joy sticking a hot poker up his ass. Who am I kidding—what's love got to do with anything?"

"Do it tonight," I say. "Just zero in and remember to have fun."

"I don't know if I can. It's been so long since I've been with anyone else."

"I don't think you're going to have any problems."

Week two. Still no Frank. The longer he doesn't call, the more preoccupied I become, if for no other reason than wanting the privilege of breaking up with him. Every time the phone rings, my heart palpitates. I rent *Walking and Talking*, *Singles*, *Reality Bites*, *When Harry Met Sally*, and watch them over and over again. I've begun keeping a journal in which I give voice to what I think went wrong between us, why Frank isn't for me. I pick apart his defects and decide that underneath it all, he's just a scared little boy who smokes too much pot. This verdict, I think, is quite generous of me.

As I write, I start to consider the positives: how strong I am, and attractive, and how any guy in his right mind would be happy to have me. And if Frank can't see what a good thing he had, if a loser like him didn't get to know me well enough to appreciate my fine sense of humor and intellect, well then— FUCK HIM!!!

◦ ◦ ◦

Gustav shows up at my place with an enormous Balducci's bag filled with two *magrets de canard*, a tin of green peppercorns, a carton of cream, new potatoes, flour, butter, broccoli rabe, and a medium-size white box tied with red string. He's going to make me dinner, and he doesn't want any help. All I need to do is sit back, drink a glass of champagne, and "Let the magician perform-eh."

When I called him and told him I was feeling melancholy

about Frank, and my self-imposed lack of a job, and my living situation, and my credit-card debt, he told me to sit tight, and here he is. With bells on.

I watch him work, slicing the new potatoes fine on a mandolin and layering them symmetrically in a casserole dish with cream and Gruyère. He is methodical. After the oven has been preheating for twenty minutes, the potatoes go in. He scores the fat on the top of the duck *magrets*, covers them with plastic, and puts them in the fridge, then washes and trims the broccoli rabe. I stand by, swirling champagne bubbles on my tongue, noting his expertise. He handles food as though it were alive— delicately moving the *magrets* from their vacuum packaging as though they were chicks, and using a deft yet careful touch with the greens.

Watching Gustav makes me feel insecure about how much more I need to learn. He's got so much confidence and talent that he does all this while giving a running monologue about his recent exploits with Gem. The more he talks, the sadder I become, because it sounds like things are stellar between them.

He finally concludes with the information that "She said yes-eh."

"What do you mean, she said *yes-eh*?"

"To marrying me!" Gustav is smiling and so happy that if he weren't talking, I'm sure he'd be whistling or possibly yodeling.

I try to be enthusiastic, but for reasons that I can't quite fathom, I'm crushed. "That's great," I say. And then I can't resist—"Does this mean she'll be getting a green card, too?"

"Oh, she already has hers," Gustav says.

So it's not about the green card. "Gustav, I know you're really into her, but isn't this kind of sudden? I mean, how long have you been going out now?" My motives are not completely pure. *I can't believe that everyone I know, practically, is getting married.* And the thing that gets me the most—that I'm now beginning to understand and see clearly, as he checks the potatoes in the oven with a sharp paring knife—is I can't stand how happy he is.

"Two months? Look, babe. I know what I like. When I'm sure, I'm sure," Gustav says without an ounce of hesitation in his voice.

I think about what a gift it must be to know, so certainly, what it is you like, then to go for it and get it.

"I can't argue with that," I say, finishing off my champagne and pouring another glass. This evening, week, month, year, actually, are not going my way. I'm so upset about Gustav that I become sullen and down the full glass of bubbles in several gulps, burping quietly at the end.

"Hey, save some for me!" Gustav says, pulling a small glass container out of the Balducci's bag that looks to be—is it? Foie gras, uncut. He must have spent a fortune. Pulling pieces of toast out of the oven, he cuts off the crusts and chops them on the diagonal, making points. Arranging them on a plate with the foie and a small knife in the center, he pours himself a glass of champagne, sets the plate on the coffee table, and says, "Now I can relax for a minute."

I love foie gras, and Gustav knows this. He spreads a large pink-and-beige chunk on a toast point and hands it to me, watching me devour it with pleasure on his face. The dinner is delicious—the *poivre* sauce is perfect with the medium-rare duck, which cuts like butter. The potatoes are creamy, well seasoned, and cheesy, the rabe bright green, *croquant* and garlicky. Gustav has brought along a bottle of Cru Bourgeois, and I'm drinking it like grape juice.

Dessert is an assortment of small tarts—vanilla crème brûlée with a chocolate crust, key lime, and pear. I barely let Gustav get a fork in edgewise as I take large bites of each. Gustav sets a metal espresso maker on top of the stove, and I teeter over to the cabinet under the sink to retrieve the Courvoisier.

"Digestives! Good idea, babe."

Can Gustav tell I'm getting snockered? I've hit the point of no return—feeling good and numb. For a while I forget about Gustav and Gem, and even Frank. But after my third glass of Courvoisier, I become maudlin. "Why didn't he want me, Gustav?" I ask, hoping he'll have the answer.

"Oh, babe. Don't worry about it. Easy come, easy go, right?" he says, stroking my arm.

"But I wanted him to like me." I am drunk, whiny, sad.

"I'm sure he must have liked you, babe. Come on! He'd be crazy not to, ah? But sometimes things just aren't meant to be, you know? Remember that girl Suzy I used to go out with? That bitch from South America?"

"Vaguely."

"Well, we fought all the time. She was very jealous."

"I didn't know that."

"Yes, she was even jealous of you!" He says this with a note of outrage—like, how patently absurd.

"She was?"

Gustav is nodding.

"But there was never anything for her to be jealous of."

"I know-eh. That's what I tried to tell her."

"And?"

"Oh, it's all, how do you say? Water through the bridge?"

He cannot let it go at that. I'll take anything I can get at this point, even some ex-girlfriend's misguided jealousy. "I want to know, Gustav. Can you at least humor me?"

"Remember the time you came over to Perla to pick up that venny tenderloin?"

"Yeah."

"And she was there?"

"Yeah."

"And we were joking around with each other like we always do-eh?"

"Uh-huh."

"That was it. She said she could see there was this chemistry between us, and she was positive we'd slept together. But she was cuckoo," he says, twirling his finger up by his head. "I told her not to be so stupid-eh."

Gustav's face is beginning to lose its vertical hold, and all of a sudden I'm not feeling high or maudlin—I'm going to be sick. I lurch from the table, thinking only of getting to the toilet on time.

"Hey! Was the food that bad?" Gustav calls behind me.

Slamming the door to the bathroom, I fall to my knees in drunken prayer and reach for my hair, then realize there's nothing to pull back. I spit a couple of times, a strand of saliva stretching from my lip and hanging while I take in the scent of the cool clean ceramic. The contents of my stomach lurch up in waves. I hear a knock at the door. "Babe? You okay in there?"

"Yes. I'm fine. I don't want you to come in." The door is right next to the toilet. I'm blocking it with my crouched body, but I can feel it pressing against the side of my butt. When I turn my head up to the door, I can see Gustav's concerned face.

"I'm coming in-eh."

Flushing quickly, I rip off a large strip of toilet paper and begin wiping the rim and inside of the bowl. Gustav kneels next to me, gently rubbing my back. I'm still staring into the bowl, waiting for the next round. "I really don't want you in here," I say, but his hand stroking my back has a calming effect. He's speaking softly, saying, "It's going to be okay, babe. You're going to be fine-eh."

I throw up twice more. Relief blankets me when I'm finally done. I'm not dizzy any more, and part of me is even glad to have done away with several thousand calories. I pull out the toilet brush and Comet, and Gustav says, "I'll do that."

So while he cleans the toilet, I floss, rinse with Listerine, and brush my teeth. Afterwards, we stand side by side, looking at each other in the bathroom mirror. We are quiet. I look like hell. From the back of my head, Gustav's rabbit-eared fingers slowly emerge.

o o o

I decide if that asshole isn't going to call me, I'm going to call him. If only to give him a piece of my mind. Call me a glutton for punishment. This is probably a mistake—no, definitely a mistake, but I hope that venting will make me feel better. Give me some "closure."

Gathering courage, I pour myself a glass of white wine, slug it down, and dial. Amazingly, Frank answers, something that has never happened before. He says, "Oh, hi," all stilted and uncomfortable, and my bravado seeps from my body.

"I wanted to see how you were doing," I say.

"Oh, fine, I'm great. You?"

"Terrific!"

"That's good."

He's being so choppy and weird that I have to ask, "Do you have company?"

"Yes, as a matter of fact, yes."

"A woman?"

"Yes."

I'm seized. "Are you serious?"

"Yes. I have a friend visiting from L.A."

"You have got to be joking."

"No." He cups the mouthpiece and says in a low voice, "She's going through a rough time. Her dog just died."

Therefore she had to fly across the country to be comforted by you? This makes very little sense, but if it's a sympathy ploy, it works. The wind blows out of my sails, and I no longer feel like ripping Frank a new asshole. I just want to get off the phone and cry. I say, "Enjoy your visit."

"Thanks," he says.

It takes a while for this conversation to sink in. Really, really sink in. But when it does, I decide that Frank is a sneaky little bastard. In fact, I'm sure the only reason he even answered the phone was so that she, whoever she is, wouldn't hear my voice when the machine picked up. For all I know, that Pantene hair gel was hers. I'm way more crushed than I ought to be, logically speaking, and it makes me angry that I let someone like Frank hurt me, cause all of this anguish, lack of appetite, and all-around malaise.

The phone rings, and my heart beats wildly. What if it's Frank? Calling to apologize? *Fat chance.* A woman's voice says, "Oh, hi,

Layla, this is Patsy McLure at the Cooking Channel. We re-
ceived your résumé this week, and I was wondering if you'd be
interested in coming in for an interview."

I'm too shocked to pick up the phone.

"Aah, but I guess you're not there, so give me a call at 212-
555-1966 when you get a chance, and hopefully we'll be able to
set something up. Thanks. I'll talk to you soon."

This is totally unexpected. Someone actually wants to interview me solely on the basis of my résumé? Admittedly, a
slightly doctored résumé, but nonetheless. It's unprecedented!
I dial her number back immediately.

Patsy McLure asks if I can come in tomorrow at one o'clock.
Can I?

○ ○ ○

Patsy McLure is short and stocky with thick, medium-length
gray-blond hair. She is sweet and unthreatening and looks like
she could just as easily be baking pies in Iowa as running the
Cooking Channel. Noel she's not. She shows me around the
kitchen, introducing me to the other cooks before taking me to
the set where various cooking shows take place.

The atmosphere in the kitchen is casual; there are three
women cooking. None of them are stressed or beleaguered.
They're chatting away as if they're preparing a meal in their
own homes. There's something kind of rinky-dink about it, but
after all, they're not pumping out meals in a restaurant, merely
putting together the mise en place for the chefs who have
shows on the channel.

The cooks are chopping TV-perfect carrot cubes and onions,
measuring out butter and stock, covering the pretty glass mea-

suring cups and bowls with plastic. One woman is putting together the first stages of a jambalaya, another is preparing the
jambalaya to its halfway point, and the third is constructing
the finished jambalaya, placing pieces of sausage and craw-
dads around the fire-red Le Creuset casserole.

I will be paid $25 an hour to work eight hours a day, double
the amount I was making at Tacoma.

On my second day of work, after we've finished all the mise
en place for Mavis Delacroix's Belle of the Kitchen, she comes
in to inspect our work. She has frosty, well-coiffed blond hair
that looks like a mushroom, bright red lips, and Sally Jesse
Raphael–style glasses. She doesn't say much to us, just looks to
be sure we've made everything as picture-perfect as possible.

There is a television set up in one corner of the kitchen
where we can watch Mavis's show as it's filmed live. When the
camera does a close-up on her chopping an onion, I notice that
her nails are long and painted the same red as her lips. She
wears huge gemstones on three of the five fingers on each
hand. Whenever there's a noise offstage, she flirtatiously says,
"Whoops! Dropped ma diamond" in a kind of iambic rhythm.
You'd think that a grande dame of the kitchen such as Mavis
Delacroix, who has written several cookbooks and hosts her
own show, would have some fancy knifework to show for herself, but her nails are far too important.

By my third day in the Cooking Channel's kitchens, brui-
noising carrots with geometric perfection, measuring out
tablespoons of butter, and arranging dishes cooked from beginning, middle, and end, I'm becoming very bored indeed. I
try to turn this around by thinking of chopping as meditation,
but this goes only so far.

The other women in the kitchen are nice, but they're all ei-

ther engaged or married and have taken this job to fill the in-
terim between being engaged or married and having children.
They're all impressed that I've worked in actual restaurant
kitchens. "I don't think I could do that," one of them says.
She's not going to get any argument from me.

As much of a relief as it is to work in an environment with little pressure and no men, the Cooking Channel is the sort of
place where you could toil into your old age without being noticed or appreciated for your fine dicing skills and artistic fish
styling. It is more a way station than a career. Moreover, being
around these nice women in their secure relationships only
amplifies my immaturity and all-around lack of success as a
human being.

The atmosphere is pleasant enough, though. We talk about
our various histories, where we grew up and went to school. We
speak of girly things, like where to get highlights and who
has the best gynecologist. They tell me about their husbands
or soon-to-be husbands, and I tell them about the jokers in
my past. They have potential mates for me—brothers, friends,
cousins, school chums. One of the women asks me if I'm related to Julia Mitchner, and I tell her no.

We all focus on the screen as Mavis Delacroix pulls a pan
of fried catfish (which I have battered and fried to a golden-
sheened perfection) out of the oven and says, "Now, that's
what Mavis Delacroix calls finga-lickin' good," and winks at the
camera before the audience breaks into loud applause.

I simply cannot believe what a success this woman has made
of herself.

o o o

I take the 1 train up to West Seventy-ninth Street and walk across Central Park. It is late April, and the daffodils have sprouted in little clumps on the wet green hills. There are cyclists doing laps around the 6.1-mile loop, and joggers of all description out being good and healthy. I should be running, too, but I'm hungover from drinking a bottle of Beaujolais Nouveau and eating a gigundo Cadbury Fruit & Nut bar while blubbering over a teary Lifetime special starring Dolly Parton last night. I never knew how awesome she was—singing, acting—and that body! She's really something. But now I can't wait to get back to Tenth Street and take a nap.

There is a large wooden door at street level, with "151 East Seventy-ninth Street" scripted in gold at the top. Ringing the bell I wait, watching wealthy women around my age walking with large bags from Saks Fifth Avenue and Grace's Market. They're dressed to the hilt in expensive lightweight coats, toe-crushing pumps, and big dark glasses. Their hair is blown out and highlighted. How do they do it? Where does this wealth come from? Are they all hugely successful in their amazing careers? Married to rich guys? *Criminals?* Dressed in old Levi's and sneakers, my hair sticking out in all directions, I look like a bum who got off at the wrong subway stop.

The door is opened by a plump, sixtyish woman with long gray hair. Thick silver and turquoise bracelets travel up both arms from wrist to elbow. "You must be Layla," she says, her voice smooth as butter. She's bronzed, with laugh lines in the corners of her eyes and mouth. "I'm Dory," she says, holding out her hand and firmly shaking mine. "Come on in!"

She is not what I was expecting. Leading me into a cozy sitting room, she holds out her hand, indicating a large leather

couch across from her matching leather armchair. The furni-
ture is the color of a chestnut horse, as smooth and soft. Un-
consciously, I start stroking it. Wood burns in the fireplace,
giving the room fragrant warmth. The place smells like lemons
and trees. It looks like a Ralph Lauren ad.

Dory Windsor sits looking at me for a moment, startling me
when she jumps up and says, "I'm sorry. What can I get for you?
Sometimes I can be such a space cadet. Have you had lunch
yet?"

I haven't eaten anything today, but I say, "Oh, yes, I have,
thanks."

"Well, how about some tea or something? A glass of sherry,
perhaps?"

A glass of sherry sounds like just the ticket, but I say, "Some
tea would be wonderful."

Jerking her head to the side, she gamely says, "Follow me."

The kitchen is not what you'd call "professionally equipped."
The knives, some of them rusted, could use a good sharpening, and a couple of the iron skillets look like throwbacks from
the Civil War, but the situation isn't dire. I've got my own
knives, and several roasting and sauté pans as well.

The dining room is surrounded by oil paintings that look
suspiciously van Goghesque. There is an enormous, thick oak
table surrounded by matching oak chairs, with a cherry-wood
hutch in which I notice several bottles of top-shelf liquor, along
with crystal decanters, glasses, and goblets of every description.

"This is where I do most of my entertaining," she says. "I just
love to cook. How lucky you are to be able to make money
doing it."

I give her a weak smile. I'm not sure I share her enthusiasm.

She arranges several large homemade oatmeal, peanut-butter, and chocolate-chip cookies on a plate and turns on the electric kettle, which boils the water in sixty seconds flat. "Earl Grey okay?"

I nod.

"Milk and sugar?"

"Just milk, thanks."

We're sipping tea in the leather sitting room, and I'm waiting for her to grill me on my catering qualifications when she asks, "So tell me about yourself. Your hopes and dreams."

I'm taken off guard. I don't have any good answers to this question, so I say, "I'm not sure if I know."

"That's okay. You're still young. You may not have discovered what your dreams are yet. Or maybe you've already fulfilled certain dreams and haven't come up with new ones yet."

"I don't feel that young," I say.

"Oh, pshaw!" she says, waving her hand dismissively. "What are you? Twenty-three? Twenty-four?"

"Twenty-eight."

"You're kidding! Well, twenty-eight's still young in my book."

"I thought I wanted to be the chef of my own restaurant, but I'm not so sure anymore. It's been discouraging. I don't want to use some kind of feminist cop-out, but it's a very male-dominated world. It's hard to move ahead." And then I surprise myself by adding, "I think I may have made a mistake."

"We all make mistakes. That's how we find our way."

This makes me feel better. I've been struggling under the misconception that everyone else in the world is a homunculus, born fully formed with preconceived destinations arrived at on schedule, with little struggle or heartache. Come to think of it, even guys like Dick, with all of their money and family connections, probably haven't had it easy.

"Maybe you'll find catering private parties more to your liking?"

"I've had good experiences so far," I say, thinking guiltily of Billy's party. "What about you?"

Dory stares into her tea and smiles. "I wanted to be a painter when I was young. But I wasn't much good at it. I worked very hard and couldn't understand why someone like myself, who appreciated good art so much—knew a lot about it, too—couldn't put to canvas what I felt in my heart and head. As you can see," she says, motioning to the watercolor on the wall behind her, the name Manet scribbled at the bottom, "I became something of a collector instead."

Does this mean I will own a lot of really good restaurants?

"Every year," she continues, "I throw my spring fling the first weekend of May. It's a butterfly celebration for those of us who hermit the winter away. I invite seventy-five of my nearest and dearest. I like to think of it as my present to them for making it through the winter. I need someone capable of making food that will welcome this crowd back into the world of the living."

"I think I can handle that," I say. As soon as I've said it, I am confident it's true.

o o o

Mavis Delacroix has been rehearsing her menu of Easter ham, fried chitlins, and lemon-meringue pie. She tells Patsy she'll need an assistant who can lift the fifteen-pound ham out of the oven and glaze it while she's "whipping the meringue into seductive pale peaks." Mavis interviews us one by one and, after squeezing my biceps like loaves of Wonder, finally decides that I'll do. I will, however, need some "heavy-duty makeup" and a "complete hair blitz."

Patsy tells me in private that she's happy I was chosen. She's dangerously close to being the first boss I've ever liked.

I hate to admit it, but I'm as excited as a schoolgirl. I can't wait to have my hair and makeup done. I daydream of Mavis Delacroix and me bantering back and forth, joking about dropping our diamonds and storing everything but the kitchen sink in Ziploc bags rather than that clunky, clumsy Tupperware. In the end, Mavis Delacroix tells the cameramen not to dillydally too long on shots that include the assistant, but I don't care. I'm going to be on live TV!

I've been informed by Marquis, the makeup artist and hair guy, not to wash my hair or face for an entire day before the shoot—I need to build up the necessary oils. In the dressing room, he looks closely at my skin tone before slathering on foundation and blush. He gets in close to tweeze stray eyebrow hair and then sets to work, mixing and building color on my eyelids. Then comes natural plummy, peachy lips and mascara. There's quite a bit of time spent with various hair products, Kiehl's Silk Groom in particular. Marquis molds and shapes, while I take in the wintergreen smell of his breath. When he's through, I barely recognize myself. I look like a different person, and I'm not sure I like her.

Mavis Delacroix stops by and says, "Now you look like a real lady."

I feel silly, but I agreed to do this, and if they want me to look like Ronald McDonald, so be it. I always thought being a lady had more to do with comportment than face paint. If makeup's all there is to it, I might actually have a shot.

During the show, I stand quietly, busying myself with chopping parsley and other herbs. When Mavis Delacroix reaches for something, I move quickly to hand it to her. The ham needs basting, and for the most part, the camera focuses on the basting itself. This is not what I had in mind.

Mavis Delacroix is whipping the egg whites for the meringue with a large whisk. She is wearing a sleeveless silk top, and the upper part of her arm is jiggling out of control. She rhapsodizes about her big white mansion in Georgia and her husband, Buford, and how this is always his one special request at Eastertime. And then she does something I'm not expecting. She says, "Layla, honey? Take over for me with this whisking, wouldya, darlin'?"

Gulp. The camera zooms in on me whisking the egg whites while Mavis points to my whisking style—stiff wrist, consistent agitation. She even rolls up the sleeve of my chef's coat to call attention to my strong arm. Cue cards go up, and the audience applauds. I flex playfully, and there is laughter. I continue to smile and whisk—I'm a star!

"Now, why don't you put down that whisk a minute and slather up that beautifully bronzing ham?"

The camera follows me to the oven while Mavis gives a running dialogue on how you don't need to pay for expensive bottled glazes when making your own is a "snippety-snap."

The heat blasts out as I open the oven door and, using a kitchen towel, pull out the entire grill portion with the ham on top, as I've been doing throughout the show. This time, however, when I let go of the grill, the entire ham dives onto the floor in one loud clatter, hot sticky sauce splattering my coat and pants. The sound from the crash goes on forever.

"Whoops!" Mavis says. "Dropped ma *diamond!*"

I don't yell "Goddamn motherfuck!" as would be normal. Instead, out of nowhere, I pull a Jamie and say, "Dagnabbit!" Then, blowing a strand of hair that's fallen in my face, "That would be the Hope diamond."

Mavis starts chortling. "Honey, the Hope's got nothing on that diamond."

Ripping the second kitchen towel from the top of my apron, I pick up the hot glazed ham and hoist it back into the roasting pan the way a mother might handle a diaper change on a fussy baby. What the audience doesn't know is, this is the halfway ham. The finished one is in the kitchen, fully cooked and ready for its close-up.

My face gets redder as I frantically grope under the sink for the towels and 409. I can hear Mavis going over the pros and cons of the various types of gelatin that can be used for the lemon custard. One of the cameras, I notice, is following my every movement. With nothing to lose, I begin a quick dissertation on my circular scrubbing technique, noting that a toothbrush is the best way to be sure you don't miss any crevices.

During the cleanup operation, Patsy has hightailed it back to the kitchen at a speed that, given her size and shape, astonishes me. Out with the old ham, in with the new. Which, in customary fashion, has been shellacked to within an inch of its life with inedible glazes, colors, and chemicals so that it is now more sculpture than food.

I step toward the monstrosity and, like a game-show hostess, begin calling attention to the finished ham's many and wondrous qualities while Mavis narrates—"As you can see, this little piggy's cooked to perfection. The luscious dark pink color? That's the brown sugar doing its job. Notice the sheen— good golly, my mouth is watering already." She gets her face in close for the aromatic inhale. The chemical scent is so strong that she coughs involuntarily and is unable to speak.

Jumping in on autopilot, I say, "Smells like this ham's been refinished!"

There is laughter and applause. Encouraged, I rap the ham's hardened surface with the back of a spoon several times, smack my lips, and say, "*Bullet-proof* . . . Remember, the cooks on *Belle of the Kitchen* are trained professionals. Don't try this at home."

I'm fairly certain I'm about to be fired.

○ ○ ○

That night, while Jamie is giving me the lowdown on the nightmare that is her hunt for the perfect wedding dress, the phone rings. She answers and hands it to me, shrugging.

"Layla, hi."

I don't know who it is, but I don't want him to know that, so I tentatively say, "Hi."

"Do you know who this is?"

"I'll admit, I'm stumped."

"Ah, how quickly she forgets."

Still nothing.

"It's Dick Davenport."

"Dick?"

"Try not to say it like that," he says. "Listen, Layla, I saw you on *Belle of the Kitchen* today."

Not sure I want to delve too deeply into Dick's interest in food shows. "And?" is all I can think of to say.

"And I just wanted to call and congratulate you. Billy gave me your number, I hope that's okay."

"Fine," I say.

"I hardly recognized you at first. You give good TV."

"Dick, quit screwing with me."

"I'm serious!"

"Thanks. I guess."

"The apple doesn't fall too far from the tree after all."

"I don't like discussing apples and trees much," I say, upset by the comparison.

"Sorry," he says. "I know what you mean. I don't like it when people compare me to my father, either."

"It's okay," I say. "Just don't let it happen again." *What's with the ballbuster routine?*

"Anyway, I just wanted you to know I saw you and I was impressed."

"Thanks."

There's a pause. He says, "You're welcome. Have you ever thought of doing your own cooking show?"

"In my dreams."

"You should think about it. You'd be good at it."

"I appreciate your enthusiasm, but it takes a little more than desire to have your own show."

"Indeed . . ."

"Yes, indeedy."

"So, Billy tells me you're a cyclist?"

"Uh-huh," I say, hearing his call waiting click.

"Maybe we could go riding sometime?"

"Sure." *Is he asking me on a date?*

"Can you hold a minute?" he asks.

"No problem." *I hate being put on friggin' hold!*

He comes back several seconds later. "Sorry about that."

"Not a problem," I say, hoping my voice doesn't betray me.

"Hey, by the way, thanks for that champagne. Did you get my note?"

"Yes, I did, thanks. It was my pleasure. You looked like you needed it."

I can hear more clicking from his call waiting. "Do you need to get that?"

"Yeah, I think I should. I'm in the middle of this work thing. I'll give you a call about that bike ride."

"Yeah, okay." *Just don't ask me to hold my breath.*

"Right. Okay, then. Good-bye."

"Good-bye."

"Who was that?" Jamie asks.

"Oh, just this guy, Dick, that Billy tried to set me up with."

"Hm. Dick what?"

"Davenport."

"*Dick Davenport Dick Davenport?*"

"Yup."

"Is calling you?

"He wanted to tell me I did a good job on this cooking show today."

"You were on a cooking show today?"

"Yeah, *Belle of the Kitchen.*"

"With Mavis Delacroix?"

"That's the one."

"Oh my goodness," she says, putting her hand delicately in front of her mouth, "I *love* that show."

"That figures," I say.

Jamie lightly slaps my arm. "So he called you especially?"

"Is that weird?"

"*I'd* say. I mean, Dick Davenport's a busy guy."

"He's sort of a friend of a friend. I've been running into him a lot lately, so it's not as out of left field as it might look."

"Um, sweetie? You do know Dick Davenport *owns* the Cooking Channel?"

"Jesus Christ." *Gee, Layla, maybe you should tell Dick exactly what it takes to have your own show.* "Uh, no, actually, I didn't know that."

"Tom does some legal work for him."

"Oh yeah?"

"Yeah. Says he's a really nice, down-to-earth guy, for someone who's loaded. I'm sure it's not easy, coming from that family. Those Davenports aren't exactly a bowl of cherries, from what I hear. But I get the feeling Dick's going out of his way to break the mold."

"Meaning?"

"Haven't you read about any of this? They found his mother swimming half naked in the Duck Pond a couple of years ago. She's spent more time up at Silver Hill than anyone I know. Not that it's hard to understand. If I was married to Clive Davenport, I might go off the deep end myself. He's a shark. And there's a lot of pressure on Dick to keep the corporation running smoothly. . . ."

"Okay. I think that's a little more information than I needed."

"You asked," she says.

"Well, I'm glad to hear he's breaking the mold. Breaking the mold is good, breaking the mold is gutsy," I say, realizing that Dick and I may have more in common than I thought.

"Excuse me?" Jamie says, smiling playfully.

Shrugging, I decide to put a lid on it. I'm starting to scare myself.

○ ○ ○

I ask Gustav if he wants to make $500 helping me cater Dory's spring fling.

He says, "Yah, sure," without hesitation.

I say, "Don't you want to discuss it first?"

He says, "Don't be foolish-eh. I'd sell my mother for five hundred dollars."

"Charming."

Gustav and I begin working out the menu. Oscar agrees to add our ingredients in with his so that we can get everything wholesale. I can think of nothing else for two weeks prior. I have nightmares in which there are large rooms full of hungry people waiting for something, anything, to eat, and I'm running around like a spaz, unable to produce.

Gustav, on the other hand, is chill. He has the utmost confidence that this is going to be a career-making party for us. "This is how businesses get started," he says to me one day when we're sitting in Dory's kitchen, working out which pans, platters, and serving dishes to use for what. "Do you realize how many bigwigs are going to be at this party?"

I don't like to think of things that way, but he does have a point. "So what are you thinking, that other people will want to hire us?"

"Sure! If we do an excellent job, why wouldn't they?"

"I don't know. I don't like to take advantage."

"Babe, this isn't about taking advantage, it's about your career. This is the way it works, ah?"

"I guess so."

Shopping at D'Agostino's, I pick up a copy of TV *Guide* and discover *Intrigues* has been canned. Which is probably why Julia hasn't called in a while. I know she's alive, because she cashed the check for $750 I sent her a week ago. I toy with calling her, as she tends to be much nicer and more humble when she's out of work, but decide to hold off. I don't want to shatter the small amount of confidence I've managed to gain over the last couple of weeks.

I meet with Dory to go over things before the party, and we wind up talking about everything *but* the party over a bottle of good wine and take-out Chinese. The Frank fiasco doesn't shock or surprise her. When I tell her the part about the hand-cuffs, she waves her hand and says, "That's nothing. When I lived in Sedona, I fell in love with a Planetarian guru who tied me to a pole surrounded by sage, which he lit to attract extra-terrestrials."

I am transfixed.

"Oh, yes, he had a whole cult following. None of them knew he was addicted to peyote. The man was crazy as a coconut, but I was mad for him. I would have done anything he asked. Well," she says, chuckling to herself and sipping her wine, "maybe not *anything*." She gets a pensive look on her face. "Yes, now that I think about it, I would have done absolutely anything. . . . As you grow older, things you've done in the past can seem silly and naive, but I've always thought of my ridiculous past as a good learning experience. I think the trick is to accept who you are and not penalize yourself too much."

"Right," I say, clinking my glass on hers. After taking a sip of wine, I say, "I would like to have a decent relationship with a man at some point, though."

"Oh, you say that now, but just wait. When I was alone, there was nothing that I wanted more than a man, but after twenty years of marriage, I couldn't wait to get rid of him. I've found I've been living very happily without a man since my husband left."

"You haven't had any suitors? Boyfriends?"

"Oh, well," she says, "Chin and I sleep together on occasion."

"Who's Chin?"

"My housekeeper," she says airily. "He's more of a friend, really."

o o o

I've started riding my bike up to Central Park, in order to run the loop on Saturday mornings. I always see an older man with wild white Einstein hair, tanned skin, and a perpetual smile hanging out by the reservoir. Ripped, faded newspaper articles posted by the water fountains call him the Mayor of Central Park. He used to run marathons, and when he stopped running, he started walking down to the reservoir every day from where he lives in the Bronx. I look forward to seeing him. We wave to each other. I like to think that he distinguishes me from the rest of the joggers he waves to.

My hair has grown out a little, and I'm starting to look and feel like a girl again.

I'm running along the dirt path around the reservoir. The May weather is beautiful—sunny and warm—and everyone in the park looks like the weight of winter has been lifted from their shoulders. There is a film of sweat covering my bare arms and legs. The endorphins have kicked in, and I'm feeling deliriously good.

One of my laces has come undone. Bending down to tie it, I

glance toward the carriage path twenty feet away and spot an attractive-looking couple. They are walking side by side, chatting animatedly, lovers staving off loneliness, sharing a Hallmark moment on a beautiful day in the park. Evidently, this is not my lot.

I'm outright gawking now. The longer I stare, the more familiar they become. Dick and Lucinda? *Figures.* He's dressed casually in khakis and sneakers. She's decked to the nines in a flowery dress, a silk scarf tied coquettishly around her head—a new bohemian. She looks about to break an ankle in what look to be a pair of low-heeled mules.

I am paralyzed in my bent position, my mouth hanging open—if it weren't so dry, I'd probably be drooling. Joggers are passing, kicking up more dirt than they need to, giving me disapproving looks. I'm ruining the whole flow of things on the path.

A pang of something shoots through my chest—something I'm finding difficult to identify. I cannot be falling for Dick. Impossible! There are some things about him that are okay, I guess, but he doesn't seem to have very good taste in women. *My God, he's looking right at me!*

A flash of recognition passes over his face, and his eyes soften. He puts his hand up to the side of his head, thumb and pinky extended. Does he have an itch?

I am up and running.

As I unlock my bike from the rod-iron fence at the south end of the park, I notice the back tire's flat. You'd think by now I'd be smart enough to carry a pump and patch kit, but noooo. I've got to wing it. Take my chances. And what happens when you take chances? Clearly, you get screwed. Sitting on the 1 train heading downtown, the front wheel of my bike wedged against my foot, I wipe the dirt off the inside of my lower calves. I am numb with exhaustion. All I can think of is how good that Gatorade is going to taste when I get off and hit the deli. I'm staring at the floor of the subway, the sneakers, sandals, and shoes, the books that people are reading, going over the ingredients for Dory's party, *Got to call the florist, the table and dinnerware rental place. . . . Dory's taking care of place cards. . . .*

I *do* have a life, even if I don't have a boyfriend.

The message light is blinking when I get home. "Hey, Layla, it's Dick. I saw you in the park, I don't know if you saw me? Anyway, I wanted to see if you were still interested in going on that bike ride. . . ."

"Maybe Lucinda would like to join?" I angrily ask over his voice.

". . . let me know."

o o o

A week later, on Monday morning, I am dicing onions in the Cooking Channel kitchen, nose running, tears dribbling down the side of my face, when I blurrily notice Patsy McLure in the hallway talking to someone tall, with short dark hair. Soon they are standing in the doorway, and Patsy is saying, "Everyone? I'd like to introduce you to Dick Davenport, owner of the Cooking Channel."

Even the married girls look like they're flirting when they smile and say, "Hi." *So he's not bad-looking. Big deal.*

Dick walks up and hands me a monogrammed handkerchief. "What's the matter, sad you never called me back?"

Ignoring him, I continue to chop and sniffle.

"Well, you must be upset about *something*," he says, sounding cheery.

"They're called onions," I say, muttering "asshole" under my breath.

"Hey, hey!" he says, holding up his hands. "Can we take this outside?"

"Can't you see I'm busy?"

"Outside." He says, jerking his head toward the door.

Slamming my knife on the cutting board, I follow him out into the hallway. I am so *over* being some guy's second choice. "What," I say, facing him.

"You did see me in the park, didn't you? You saw me walking with Lucinda."

If he doesn't wipe that smug smile off his face . . . "Yeah? So? So you have a girlfriend, why are you calling me?"

"First of all, she's not my girlfriend anymore," he says seriously. "And secondly, I'm calling you because I like you and would like to spend more time with you. Is that all right?"

"You and Lucinda broke up?" I ask, my voice sounding a bit too hopeful.

"A while ago."

"Care to give a month count?"

"You mean an hour count?"

"You are such a pig," I say, turning on my heel.

"Ho, ho, hooold on a minute there," he says, putting his hand on my shoulder. "That was my lame attempt at humor, but I can see you are not amused. It's been three months now," he says, holding up the corresponding fingers.

"And you still take walks together in the park?"

"Believe it or not, we're still friends."

"That's awfully mature of you."

"Yes, it is," he says, making me feel childish.

"Okay," I say.

"Okay what?"

"Okay, I'll go for a bike ride with you. But that is it!" I'm smiling now.

"How about a bike ride and a hot dog?"

"We'll see."

"Maybe a Coke?"

"Don't push your luck."

о о о

Gustav and I arrange everything ahead of time so it will all be ready when the guests arrive. The only things we'll need to do are heat the various hors d'oeuvres and make sure everything's timed right, looking perfect, before it leaves the kitchen. Dory has hired a virtual battalion of servers, all dressed traditionally in black coats and ties, even the women. There are two dishwashers to clean plates and platters as they come back into the kitchen.

Gustav and I are dressed in checked pants and brand-new white chef's coats, with folded white scarves around our necks and toques on our heads. We're working well together. Gustav not only refrains from bossing me around, he actually takes orders a couple of times without imitating my girly voice.

Billy comes into the kitchen wearing a tux with a flowery Liberty cummerbund and bow tie. Miguel is at his side, wearing a more staid tux, with a soft peach shirt and tie. They make a great-looking couple. "And lookee, lookee here," Billy says, "I see you're settling right into the Windsor kitchen."

I'm in concentration mode, arranging warm phyllo triangles stuffed with blue cheese and walnuts on doilied platters.

"I take it you and Dory are getting along?"

"Billy," I say, keeping my eyes on my work, "not now."

Pinching a triangle from the tray, he says, "Don't mind if I do. Miguel? Come here, let me feed you."

Slightly taller than Billy, Miguel has to bend down to receive his bite, almost like an altar boy taking communion. "Delicee-yooze," he says, in Portuguese-accented French.

When Miguel is done savoring, Billy pops the rest in his mouth, saying, "You've really outdone yourself this time."

"Thanks-eh," Gustav cuts in. "And now she needs to start spooning caviar on these blinis."

"Come out when you're through, okay?"

The dinner is a smashing success. Gustav and I are exhausted when we head out into the dining room. We've taken off our toques. Crystal is tapped. "Everyone! Everyone! Silence, please!" It's Dory. Now I know where Billy got his habit. All of the conversations hush to a murmur and then total silence. Standing, letting the silence give poignancy to what she is about to say, Dory exclaims, "Please meet Layla Mitchner and Gustav Marcam, the chefs!"

A loud round of applause. Cheers of "Hear, hear!" More silver tinkling crystal. I look out into a sea of faces. Everything is a blur, a happy adrenaline rush. Gustav grabs my hand, raises it up, and like we're actors taking our curtain call, we bow.

As I come up, one face in the crowd catches my attention.

Our eyes lock and he's up, moving toward me. A small group of middle-aged women zero in on Gustav, while the rest of the guests return to their conversation. "You're everywhere these days, aren't you?" Dick Davenport asks.

"Are you stalking me?"

"Actually, Dory's my godmother. I've been attending the spring fling since I was able to walk. . . . So you're moonlighting?"

"I'm trying to keep my apartment after my roommate moves out."

"A real go-getter. I like that," he says, looking like he means it.

I wouldn't exactly classify myself as a go-getter, but I'm happy to allow Dick his illusion. Standing before me in his tux, he cuts a strapping figure, making me wish I had on something a little more feminine.

"You look great in your uniform," Dick says, as if reading my mind.

"Thanks. You don't look half bad in that penguin suit."

Adjusting his bow tie and looking somewhat sheepish, he says, "I hate these things. . . . So there's something I've been meaning to talk to you about."

"Fire away."

"Let's go to the kitchen," he says, taking me by the arm. Pulling a pack of cigarettes out of his pocket, he knocks one up, and I take it from the pack. Lighting it for me, he says, "Can we share that one? I'm not really a smoker."

"Neither am I," I say, inhaling and handing it to him.

Taking a drag, he hands it back and asks, "Did you make that apple tart?"

"Yup."

Dick nods, a pensive look on his face, like he's taking a mental note.

"You hated it," I say, my heart beating double time.

"No," he says, shaking his head solemnly, looking down at the floor.

"The crust wasn't flaky enough," I say, ticking off the tart's pitfalls, "and the vanilla cream could have been sweeter, I know, and I was going for more of a homestyle look—"

"Layla," Dick says, putting his hand on my wrist, "will you shut up, please?"

"Look, I had a lot of things to think about tonight, and I'm sorry if the dessert wasn't up to Davenportian standards. . . ."

"It was excellent," he says simply.

"Oh," I mumble, embarrassed. "Thank you."

"And that goes for everything else on the menu tonight."

"Yeah, well, the Béarnaise did start breaking up at the end—"

"You better start learning to accept compliments," he says.

"I had help," I say.

"Have you thought any more about having your own show?"

"Like I told you, only in my dreams."

"I'd like you to put together a proposal for a cooking pilot."

"Really?"

"Yes, really. The ratings for *Belle of the Kitchen* went through the roof the day you were on. It was reality food TV—I'm convinced we're looking at a new genre. You seem pretty outdoorsy; think outside the box. Get something to me by the end of the week, and we'll discuss it."

In my enthusiasm, I want to blurt, *No fucking way!* Instead, thank God, I hold it together and coolly reply, "Aye-aye, Captain."

"Who is smoking in my kitchen?" Dory says, walking through the service door with a glass of port.

Dick hands her a cigarette and lights it. Taking a long drag, she says, "One of life's great pleasures."

"You're still only smoking one a day, though, right?" Dick asks.

"That's right, sonny, everything in moderation. So I was thinking, Layla," she says, pausing to blow out a cool line of smoke, looking at me sideways, "if you two wanted to go out and grab a drink, I could lend you something to wear."

Dick says, "She looks great the way she is."

Gustav grunts. "I'm not sure what that says about you."

"What size are your feet?" Dory asks.

"Nine."

"Perfect," she says, "Follow me."

"I used to be quite a looker, if you can believe it," she says when we're standing in her enormous closet, surrounded by racks of dresses, pantsuits, and an Imelda Marcos–sized shoe collection. "Never thrown out a dress in my life." She is rummaging through yards of silk, wool, and cashmere with one hand, her glass of port in the other. I am sitting on the floor in my soiled chef's jacket and underwear, giving my sore feet a rest, breathing in the smell of fabric and fading perfume.

Dory turns from the clothes abruptly and says, "Dick is a wonderful young man. I want him to be happy."

"He looks pretty happy to me," I say.

"He hasn't had it easy," she says quietly, almost to herself.

I'm just about to ask her what exactly is wrong with Dick

Davenport when she cheerily says, "Voilà! This is the one I think would be perfect on you."

"Who is that?" I say, staring at myself in the mirror. I am wearing a sleeveless silk chiffon dress that hugs and flutters, in a light shade of blue that matches my eyes. The back is low-cut, and the front scoops my chest in a way that makes me look better endowed than I am. The pumps, although high, are a comfortable, soft, pale tan leather.

Dick is sitting in the kitchen smoking a cigarette with Gustav when Dory and I walk in. Looking up at the same time, they stop talking.

I look ridiculous . . .

"Babe—" Gustav says.

"What he said," Dick says.

"Hey-eh, maybe you two better skip the drink and get a room," Gustav says.

I shoot him a look.

"What? I just call it like I see it-eh."

"So where's it going to be, kids? The Carlyle?" Dory asks, taking a drag off Dick's cigarette.

"I don't know. Layla? How does the Carlyle sound to you?"

Not exactly funky, not particularly hip, but for some reason, I want to have a drink at the Carlyle like I've never wanted a drink anywhere else. "Sounds perfect," I say, getting lost in a quick dream sequence starring embellished versions of Dick and me sipping Bombay martinis with big green olives and whispering sweet nothings to each other. Which, come to think of it, aren't sweet nothings but significant somethings.

There is a cell phone ringing in Dick's jacket pocket, and he reaches in and takes it out of the kitchen. He looks pale when he comes back, grabs his jacket, and says, "I'm going to have to take a rain check."

"Rain check!" Dory tipsily shrieks. "What's this about rain checks?"

"Family crisis," he says, whipping into his tux coat.

What about the Carlyle? What about me? I want to ask, but he's rushing for the door, no good-byes. He does stop and glance back long enough for me to blurt, "What kind of family crisis?" My voice is not exactly sympathetic.

"I'm sorry," he says, his face saying either "Tough shit" or "Please believe me," I can't tell which.

"No biggie," I say, smiling bravely, even though I feel like crumbling to the floor in a big silk pile. *Family crisis, yeah, okay, whatever.* I look ridiculous standing here in this getup, pretending to be glamorous and pretty. This is how God punishes fakers.

Dory follows Dick to the front door. I can hear them talking softly before the heavy wood door bangs shut. There are other voices in the hallway now, kisses and farewells.

I slouch down in a metal chair next to the kitchen telephone. "And he's *outta here*," I say to no one in particular.

Gustav looks at me sympathetically and holds up a bottle of champagne, saying, "I've got just the ticket."

Staring down at the blue silk ripples fluttering around my chest, I think, *Why do I repel men?*

I hear a cork pop and feel a cold flute being placed in my hand.

"Do you buy it?" I ask.

"Do I buy what?" Gustav asks, perplexed.

"The family crisis."

"Sure, why not-eh," he says, shrugging.

"I don't know. It's just so fucking typical," I say, feelings of rejection giving way to anger. "I think that loser's ditching me!"

"Excuse me, but what is your problem?" Gustav asks, sounding slightly fed up. "Why do you immediately assume he's ditching you? Sometimes I don't think you realize the way others see you-eh."

"Oh, yes I do," I say quickly.

"You *can* be kind of a bitch."

"Right," I say, unable to keep myself from cracking a smile.

"You dress up nice, though," he says, giving me a couple of Groucho Marx eyebrow wiggles. "He seems like a good guy." Gustav takes a large gulp of champagne, smacks his lips, and burps loudly.

"Not as good as you," I say, swallowing a mouthful and burping myself.

"Ah, my darling, but no one's as good as me. If I've told you this once, I've told you a thousand times," he says, holding out his hand, pulling me into his arms, and pressing his cheek against mine in cheesy dance position. He twirls me professionally a couple of times before breaking away and handing me an apron. "You don't want to mess up that dress," he says, nodding toward several platters of tenderloin and poached salmon waiting to be put away.

Putting the apron over my head, I tie the string around my waist. This is not the way cooks usually wear aprons. Generally, even full-body aprons are folded neatly from the top down to half their size and tied around the waist, the string neatly tucked under the fold, but Gustav is right, I don't want to mess up Dory's dress.

"Let me get my clogs," I say, carefully removing the pumps and placing them on top of a kitchen cabinet. I take the winding stairs up to Dory's room, rather than the elevator, to give myself some time to think, gain some composure. *Family crisis, family crisis ... How stupid does he think I am?* I guess I should feel grateful that he blew me off before things had a chance to get ugly. Shouldn't I know by now that I'm just not destined to be in a relationship? There are plenty of cool women who went through life alone, weren't there? Georgia O'Keeffe—no, she was married. . . . Flannery O'Connor—but I guess she died young. . . .

When I get back to the kitchen, Gustav is standing at the sink, washing his knives. The counter is neatly wiped down. "Dory says we can take the leftovers home," he says over his shoulder. "I packed you a bag."

"Thanks, Gustav."

"Babe?" he says, turning from the sink to face me, "don't worry too much about that guy, okay-eh?"

Moving toward the sink, I'm looking around for my dirty knives when I notice Gustav has already cleaned, dried, and lined them up on a fresh dry towel. "You didn't have to clean my knives," I say, thankful he did.

"Anytime, my darling."

Silently inserting our blades into the cardboard protectors, we slip them into their slots in our cases.

"Tell me I'm just being paranoid," I say, nervous despair rising in my stomach.

"Maybe you are, maybe you're not."

"Thanks. That's helpful."

"I'll tell you one thing for sure—if it's supposed to work out, it will."

"Right," I say, breathing deeply a couple of times. *Let go, let go, let go . . .*

After I take off my apron, I'm left standing in the middle of the kitchen in the dress and my sauce-spattered clogs.

"Good look, babe."

"Oh, you think so?" I say, clomping exaggeratedly over to the chair, plopping down, sticking an unlit cigarette in my mouth, and crossing my legs man-style, ankle to knee.

"Nice underwear," Gustav says. "Come on, put your pretty shoes back on, and let's finish this champagne on the balcony."

Billy and Miguel are already out there, drinking digestives out of snifters as big as small heads. The May air is soft, the breeze from the Hudson warm. Billy's face emerges from behind his glass. "Va-va-voom!" he says. And then, "So what's this I hear about someone putting together a proposal for a new cooking show?"

"Yes," Miguel says in his limited English, nodding enthusiastically.

"I don't want to talk about it," I say.

Ignoring me, Billy begins rhapsodizing. "Something casual yet adventurous, like yourself, for the young, active crowd—you again—who are too busy to cook for themselves but still enjoy learning about new things. Maybe they yearn to get out of the city, their jobs, their relationships, don't get out as much as they'd like. . . . You could travel around the world! Riding camels by day and whipping up couscous with the Bedouins at night! Bungee jumping and kangaroo burgers! Extreme skiing

and fondue! This show would allow the audience to live vicari-
ously through its host—hey! That's good! You could call the
show something like 'The Vicarious Cook'! Or, for the sexually
frustrated, 'The Vibrating Cook.' You could use vibrators instead of whisks!"

"Stop it!" I say. "Dick Davenport is not interested in me, in
any way, for any reason. And frankly," I add, somewhat less
sure of myself, "I'm not interested in him."

"Quick, Miguel, sit on your hands. You want to keep your
limbs close to your body when she gets like this," Billy says.

Miguel must understand more English than he speaks, because he quickly slides his hands under his butt.

"Dick had to leave in a hurry tonight," Gustav explains.

"Oh," Billy says, deflating. "Well, that doesn't necessarily
mean anything, does it?"

"We were just about to go to the Carlyle for drinks," I say.

"And?"

"And nothing! He had to leave, that's all."

"Something about a crisis," Gustav says.

"Crisis? What kind of crisis?" Billy asks.

"Exactly," I say, ignoring the note of concern in his voice.

"Layla, has it occurred to you that something terrible might
have happened?" Billy asks, snapping me out of my own little
world for a moment.

"No, it hasn't," I say quietly.

"Well, did he give you some kind of excuse?"

"No, he just bolted."

Sitting back and swirling the dark liquid in his snifter, Billy
looks contemplative when he says, "I am really going to enjoy
spanking that young man."

o o o

I can hear laughter as I approach the apartment door. I just don't think I can face Jamie and Tom, drinking champagne and making the most of their ideal existence right now. Slipping into the kitchen, I notice a plump letter from Julia lurking on top of the toaster. I've learned to dread these envelopes, with their slanting scrawl and little gold embossed return addresses. They always hold cautionary news items about the latest sexually transmitted diseases, or *Cosmo* stories about New York bachelors who, contrary to earnest claims, are only earnestly interested in dipping their wicks into as many beautiful, talented, and pitifully unsuspecting city girls as they can. There *are* no eligible bachelors in New York!

Pouring a large glass of water from the Brita pitcher, I gulp down half, bracing myself for the picture of bliss I am about to encounter. My feet have started hurting, but I try to buck up and look like I can sport a sexy outfit with the best of them as I strut down the short entry corridor and into the living room.

"*Here* you are!" Jamie practically screams. She's curled up like a little sex kitten on the couch. Sitting across from her on a folding chair, wearing a Butthole Surfers T-shirt and a pair of ripped jeans is Frank.

"Shiiiit," he says, slow and drawn-out.

"Fuuuuck," I say, the air leaching from my lungs.

"Sweetie, you look—"

"Hot," Frank says.

I think I'm going to faint. I've got to keep it together, try to look calm. "I need a drink," I say, pulling an about-face and heading for the kitchen.

Jamie calls out, "There's a bottle of Bushmills on the counter!"

My hand is shaking when I grab the bottle and slug back a large shot. I can hear footsteps approaching as I pour myself a stiff one on the rocks. Jamie sticks her whiskey lips next to my ear, flecking it with spit when she says, "He's a hunk!"

"A hunk of shit," I say, taking a large gulp of my drink.

"He has been gushing on about you for the last forty-five minutes. He says you broke his heart." Jamie is drunk, her voice slurred in whiny sympathy. This is what Frank does to women.

More footsteps. "We need to talk," Frank says from the doorway, looking grave.

"Say no more!" Jamie sings as she wiggles out of the kitchen. "I can take a hint!"

I can feel the heat coming off Frank's arms, but refuse to look at him. I can barely keep my knees from knocking together.

"Can't you even look at me?" Frank asks.

"No," I say, my eyes on my drink.

"Layla," Frank says, putting his hand on my bare shoulder.

Shrugging his hand off, I look him in the eye and can think of absolutely nothing to say. Is this not the moment of glory I've been waiting for?

We stand there not talking for what feels like an eternity. After taking another sip of my drink, I ask, "What can I do for you, Frank?" I ask, noticing a new silver hoop earring in his left ear.

"I need you," he says, slow and puppyish.

"You need me?" I ask. "That is so sweet."

"I know it sounds corny," Frank says, pausing, searching for his next words, "but you make me feel . . . I don't know, real or something."

"It's May, Frank. I haven't seen you since February, and the last time we talked, you had company and couldn't give me the time of day."

Frank stands there with a blank expression on his face.

"Hello?"

"Hi," he says.

"Are you stoned?"

"A little," he says, his dimples elongating.

I am so impressed by his sheer audacity that I cannot speak.

"Look," he says, "I made a mistake. It happens. I didn't know what I had when I had it," he says, holding his closed hand to his chest. "And then I lost it," releasing his fingers, palm out. "That's when I realized," pointing a finger to the side of his head, "that what I had was what I wanted in the first place."

"I think those 'NSync videos are starting to get to you." Turning to the philodendron on the windowsill, I transport it to the sink and turn on the tap.

"I still have those hyacinths," Frank says.

Even though I'm sure those hyacinths are dead as doornails by now, I'm touched. "You do?" I hear myself saying, my voice so tender I'm not sure it's me talking. I am softening. *Things with Frank weren't really so bad, were they? Are we not artists, after all? Do we not thrive on drama? Heartbreak? Insanity?*

I'm looking at him now, at his face moving in closer. I am paralyzed, drunk, my eyes closing to half slits. I can feel his warm breath on my face, and widening one eye, I am zapped by the vision of Frank, puckering up like a goofy pirate.

What am I, desperate? Pushing him back, I say, "Frank, I think you should go now," like a character on one of Julia's shows.

His mouth curls up at the sides in an "I'm sexy and you know it" smile. He says, "Come on," all cocky and sure, "you know you don't mean that."

Moving swiftly around him toward the door, I pull it open and wait for him to pass through.

He stands there looking at me like he just cannot believe what I'm saying. Like, *How can you let this studly package go?* Stepping out onto the landing and facing me, he says, "I'm not going to beg."

"Good," I say.

Standing there listening to his work boots scuffing down the stairs, I have a moment of doubt. Have I just closed the door on my last opportunity for true love?

It's six in the morning when I stumble into the living room naked, on my way to the bathroom. Jamie is lying on the couch in her Hilton bathrobe with one of those frozen blue ice packs over her eyes—her feet, propped up on a pillow, are encased in soft leather open-toed wedgie slippers. A large bottle of Advil and a big beach glass filled with water and little plastic ice fish sit on the coffee table at arm's distance. She groans softly a couple of times. "From now on, it's water and fruit juice. . . ."

Heading back into the living room wrapped in a towel, I sit on the edge of the couch, helping myself to several Advil and multiple gulps of water, sucking loudly around the plastic fish. Jamie holds up one finger and, like a soldier on a battlefield uttering her final words, says, "Check messages."

"Ungh," I mutter into the glass before stumbling back to my futon on the floor.

When I wake up three hours later, I'm so late I don't even have time for coffee. Pulling on Levi's and a T-shirt, I brush my teeth, grab my bike, and head out the door.

o o o

Patsy McLure comes into the kitchen and tells me I have a phone call. "Come and take it in my office," she says, "sounds important."

The voice on the other end of the line is low and sleepy. "Layla? I've been trying to reach you. Jamie gave me this number."

"Frank?"

"Yeah, sorry to disappoint you."

"What do you want?"

"I changed my mind. I ain't too proud to beg."

"You've gotta stop using song lyrics to express yourself."

"Layla, there were things I wanted to tell you last night, things I never got to say. Can I see you? Just to talk?"

I entertain the idea for several seconds—maybe things *could* work out between us?—before getting myself together to say, "I don't think that's a good idea."

Patsy's shuffling papers, but I can tell she's listening. She prides herself on knowing what's going on in all of her cooks' private lives.

"Five minutes," he says. "A friendly chat."

"Frank, I'm working, I've gotta go."

"Oh, come on," he says, his voice cool and sexy, "don't play me this way."

"Don't play *you* this way? Who played whom here, Frank? What's the matter, you having a dry month or something?"

"Please," he says in a voice that sounds genuinely sad. "I'm downstairs in the lobby. I'm coming up to see you."

Fuck. "No, stay right there. I'll come down." *I am such a sucker.*

After I hang up Patsy asks, "Man trouble?" as if she relates.

"You could say that," I say.

She sighs. "That's why *I'm* not married anymore."

"I've got to go downstairs for a couple of minutes," I explain. "Is that okay?"

"If you're not back up in fifteen minutes, do I have your permission to call security?" she asks, as though there's nothing she'd like to do more.

"Absolutely," I say, rushing out the door.

Down in the lobby, I say, "Frank, I don't have much time." I've left a distance of about three feet between us, but he's moving in, closing the gap.

"Can we get a cup of coffee or something?" he asks.

Jack, the burly Australian security guard, calls out to me, "How's it going today, mate?"

"Fine, thanks, and you?" I ask, trying to sound chipper, leading Frank out to the sidewalk.

"Look," I say, facing him, my back to the sun, "we're not going to get a cup of coffee."

"Can't we just discuss it?" he asks, squinting into the bright sun.

"I'm sorry, but I'm going to have to deprive you of the opportunity of fucking with me."

Frank looks down at his boots as if I've just made a good point. "I don't want to fuck *with* you. To be honest, Layla," he says, a malicious smile playing on his lips, "I just wanted to see if I could get you to come down here and talk to me. It's kind of a game I like to play with myself."

Looking up, I see Dick in the distance. He's walking at breakneck speed. I can smell the delicious scent of his freshly shaved face as he approaches. "Hey," he says, getting up close to me, vibrant and healthy. "I was hoping I'd get to see you before lunch."

"Hi," I say. *Glad you could fit me in.*

Frank taps him on the shoulder and says, "Hey, *Dick*, remember me? Layla's *boyfriend*?"

"Shut up, Frank," I say, at the end of my rope.

Dick looks bewildered, then hurt. "Yeah, you're the guy I met up in Vermont, right?" Despite the movement in his jaw indicating he'd rather eat dirt, Dick's manners prevent him from doing anything but offering Frank his hand.

"Good memory," Frank says, ignoring Dick's hand. "Anyway, I was just here to give Layla a little afternoon delight."

"You what?" Dick says, shocked yet evidently amused.

This is not the reaction Frank was hoping for. "Get her going until she cries out 'Oh God! Oh God! Oh God!' You know how she does that? Oh, sorry. I guess you wouldn't, would you? Take it from me, Dick, she's hot in the sack." Frank places his hand on the back of my neck.

I try shrugging it off, but he grips me harder.

"I think you better take your hand off her now, sport," Dick says.

"Oh, do you, *sport*? Because I think I should inform you, before you start going postal, that I have a black belt in karate." Frank roughly pulls me against him.

Looking like more of a badass than I ever would have imagined, Dick steels his voice, begins to strip off his Armani blazer, and says, "That's fine. So do I."

So does he? Impressive.

"Enough," I say, twisting myself out of Frank's grip and facing them. "Frank, I think you should leave now."

"Hey, I'm willing to call it off right here, as long as you start walking," Dick says to Frank, cool and calm.

Frank turns his gaze to the ground and looks slightly embarrassed about his behavior. Holding his hand out toward Dick, he sounds sincere when he says, "Sorry about the misunderstanding."

Dick looks at Frank's hand a moment and then takes it. "Me, too," he says.

The three of us are standing there looking at one another, like *Now what?*

"I've got to go back to work or my boss is going to kill me," I say, trying to put an end to the discomfort.

"Yeah, I should probably get going, too," Frank says. "I guess I've caused enough trouble for one day, right?"

We all laugh softly like old friends making up after an ugly fight. Looking at his watch, Dick says, "Wow, is it after one?" and bends down to pick up his briefcase. I turn toward the gigantic glass doors of the building, comforted by the familiar sight of Jack's big head and barrel chest behind the front desk. There is a thud and a grunt. Spinning around, I see Dick holding the side of his face, a trickle of blood in the corner of his mouth.

"What happened?" I shout, adrenaline surging.

"You really shouldn't have done that," Dick says, wiping the blood from the side of his mouth with the back of his hand and getting into position—knees bent, feet firmly spread apart, hands up karate-style.

Frank looks demented as he somewhat less confidently assumes the position. With one quick, smooth motion, Dick's expensive (tasselless and, I have to admit, quite stylish) leather shoe lodges itself in Frank's face. He's down for the count, flat on his back in the middle of the sidewalk.

Dick says, "You don't really know karate, do you?"

Standing up, Frank brushes himself off and says nothing.

I'm beginning to wonder if anything about Frank was true.

"Maybe you should get going, then," Dick says, his jaw clenched, looking ready to open a can of whoopass.

Attempting casual, Frank looks at me and, motioning with his head sideways, says, "I'm gonna head."

"Later," I say.

"Much," Dick adds.

Dick and I are in the elevator, but neither of us is talking. I'm stunned, and he still seems angry. As we approach the twentieth floor, I turn to him and say, "Thanks."

He says, "You're welcome. Billy told me you broke up with that guy."

I don't explain, I just say, "Yes."

"So what was he doing here?"

Why do you care? "Harassing me."

Dick breathes out heavily.

Yeah, that's me, the girl with the psychopath. . . . Rapidly changing the subject, I ask, "Are you going to tell me where you went last night, or am I to be left with my own cruel fantasies?"

"You didn't get my message," he says, looking at me straight on before the elevator doors open. He follows me out.

"What message?" I say, stopping with my back to him.

"The message I left you from the hospital?"

"You had to go to the hospital?" I ask, horrified. "Please tell me it wasn't something you ate."

"No," he says patiently, "something my father ate. He was rushed there after dinner at Chez Martine. When my mother called from the emergency room, they still hadn't figured out what was wrong."

"Oh my God, Dick, I'm so sorry. Is he okay?"

"It turns out he's allergic to white truffle oil. He's going to be fine."

"You Davenports have some pretty fancy allergies," I say, starting to grin.

"And I didn't mean to leave without giving you an explanation, but I was sort of in shock and I didn't really know whether he was going to be all right."

"I understand," I say.

"You know, not all guys are jerks," he says.

"I know," I say quietly.

"Would you have lunch with me?"

"Are you asking me on a date?"

"Yes, I'd like to take you on a date. Is that too creepy for you?"

"No, it's not creepy at all," I say, finally internalizing that not being creepy is a *good* thing. "So, what happened between you and Lucinda?" I ask.

"She ordered half a grapefruit and dry iceberg lettuce at the Steak Pub. I take it I won't have that problem with you?"

"Not if you don't wear those loafers with the tassels on them."

"Ouch," he says, and then, seeming to weigh the advantage

of spilling the beans, continues, "I was courting an advertising account. The rep was at Billy's party that night. They're horrible but surprisingly comfy."

"You do work hard, don't you?" I say, now knowing it's true.

We're standing in the hall when Patsy McLure walks up and says, "I'm sorry to bother you, Mr. Davenport, but I need to steal this young lady from you. We've got a very busy afternoon ahead of us."

She's trying to rescue me.

"Well, we've scheduled an important lunch meeting," Dick says, pulling rank.

Patsy glares at me, dubious.

"It's okay," I whisper to her, "he's one of the good guys."

Looking at Dick with renewed admiration, she tilts toward my ear and whispers, "I always thought so, too."

Patsy gives me a wink as the elevator door opens and Dick leads me back inside. Standing side by side, we make an odd-looking couple—Dick's all sleek business, and I am the uniformed help. The elevator moves quickly, the clicking of each floor the only sound. Looking down at my baggy chef's pants, secured with a plastic-wrap belt, I am momentarily seized—*what happens when he figures out who I really am?*

"We're going to be okay," he says, intuiting my thoughts, putting his hand on mine.

The panic dissolves, and I am struck even more forcefully with a sense of calm. We are suspended in time, moving away from the earth at high speed.

"Where are you taking me, Mr. Davenport?" I ask.

"Up," he says.

ABOUT THE AUTHOR

HANNAH MCCOUCH is a graduate of Columbia University's M.F.A. Writing Division and Le Cordon Bleu. She has worked as a cook in numerous restaurants and at the Television Food Network. Her writing has appeared in *Cosmopolitan, New York Press, Blue, Bikini, Word,* and the book *Gig.* She lives in Brooklyn, New York, with her husband.